A virgin…now pregnant with his baby. It was too ludicrous to even be laughable. Was he actually expected to swallow such a preposterous story?

He picked up a paperweight off his desk and rubbed the smooth stone over the palm of his hand, flexing his fingers and frowning as he replaced it.

The truth in this case was that he had been stupid, but not criminally so. They might never have made it to a bed, but he'd always had safe sex—why, even when they'd ended up on the floor…

Severo froze, every muscle in his body tense as he tried to remember.

He shook his head—was it possible?

Kim Lawrence lives on a farm in rural Anglesey. She runs two miles daily, and finds this an excellent opportunity to unwind and seek inspiration for her writing! It also helps her keep up with her husband, two active sons, and the various stray animals which have adopted them. Always a fanatical consumer of fiction, she is now equally enthusiastic about writing. She loves a happy ending!

STRANDED, SEDUCED... PREGNANT

BY
KIM LAWRENCE

MILLS & BOON

All the characters in this book have no existence outside the imagination
of the author, and have no relation whatsoever to anyone bearing the
same name or names. They are not even distantly inspired by any
individual known or unknown to the author, and all the incidents are
pure invention.

First published in Great Britain 2010
Harlequin Mills & Boon Limited,
Eton House, 18-24 Paradise Road, Richmond, Surrey TW9 1SR

© Kim Lawrence 2010

ISBN: 978 0 263 87865 3

Harlequin Mills & Boon policy is to use papers that are natural,
renewable and recyclable products and made from wood grown in
sustainable forests. The logging and manufacturing process conform
to the legal environmental regulations of the country of origin.

Printed and bound in Spain
by Litografia Rosés, S.A., Barcelona

STRANDED, SEDUCED…
PREGNANT

CHAPTER ONE

HOLDING the steaming mugs high to avoid collision, Neve smiled an apology as she backed cautiously around a large, noisy family group who had bagged a much coveted table. One of them moved a bag out of her way as Neve continued to look around for Hannah, who was not where she had left her.

The mistake, she recognized, had been saying, 'Don't move,' before she went to queue at the bar for hot drinks.

She gave a silent sigh and thought, When will I learn?

Any instruction, no matter how innocuous, and Hannah could be guaranteed to do the exact opposite—the possibility that this half-term break might be a bonding experience had never been exactly realistic, but at that moment it seemed laughable.

Neve paused, her narrowed eyes moving across the heads of the people crammed into the low-beamed room, people like herself, stranded travellers who had found sanctuary in this remote coaching inn. Her glance strayed to the leaded window, and she shivered; the blizzard that had embarrassed the weather forecasters and brought the West Country to a halt continued to rage unabated.

She breathed in to let someone squeeze past and out of the corner of her eye she caught a flash of blue. The controversial streaks in the dark glossy hair identified the head as that of her stepdaughter, who had taken possession of a wooden settle by a window.

Neve took a deep sustaining breath and began to weave her way through the crowd. She managed to reach the window without scalding anyone with their hot drinks.

'Nice work—you found a better seat.' Keep it light, Neve. 'I thought I'd lost you,' she added, placing the mugs of cocoa beside the pot of fragrant blue hyacinths on the slate window sill before pulling the hat crammed down on her auburn curls from her head.

She shook back her hair, easing free the strands that had insinuated themselves down the neck of her sweater, and peeled off her jacket. The room heated by roaring log fires at both ends was warm. 'I thought cocoa might complete the warming process, topped with cream and marshmallows—I couldn't resist!' Even to her own ears her attempt at camaraderie sounded unconvincing and slightly desperate.

Hannah clearly thought so too. Her stepdaughter flicked her a look of shrivelling contempt, of the type that it seemed to Neve only a teenager could pull off, before shrugging and ignoring the drink with a muttered, 'Do you have any idea how many calories are in that? You should be fat as a pig.'

So no lull in hostilities.

With her smile pasted in place, Neve wondered if putting on twenty pounds would make Hannah dislike her less.

Probably not. Also it would be pretty difficult: no matter what she ate her figure remained painfully skinny. She would have traded her boyish figure for feminine curves in a heartbeat, but it just was never going to happen.

The moment she sat down Hannah shuffled to the far end to avoid any possibility of physical contact. Giving her aching cheek muscles a break, Neve let her smile slip.

'Look, don't worry, I'm sure the snow will stop.'

Though it showed no sign of doing so yet, and until it did they were well and truly stuck here. Though admittedly, Neve conceded, looking around the crowded bar, there were worse places to be stranded—like outside in the snow-covered Devon moor. She shivered as she slid another look through the misted pane of the window. This was not exactly roughing it.

Hannah bounced around to face Neve and so did her glossy dark hair, complete with the blue streaks that were responsible for Neve's recent summons to the Devon school where Hannah was a weekly boarder.

Neve had responded dutifully to the summons and had sat, hands neatly folded in her lap, and listened feeling more like a pupil than a parent as the headmistress had voiced her concern—concern Neve shared.

'It's not just the hair, Mrs Macleod, or the cigarettes.' She dismissed the most recent episodes of rule breaking with a wry smile and consulted the file on her desk. 'But I do feel this situation requires attention—a united approach?'

Wondering if she looked as inadequate as she felt, Neve had nodded agreement, too worried to feel patronized. She needed all the help she could get; her parenting skills, it turned out, were zero.

'There have been any number of incidents and, as you know, not all so minor. We were very lucky that the owners of the delivery van did not choose to press charges. You do know that if it wasn't for the sad circumstances that would have been an automatic expulsion?'

'And we're very grateful,' Neve had promised her earnestly. She saw no need to mention that Hannah's 'gratitude' had taken the form of sulky silence and poisonous glares.

'It is Hannah's attitude that concerns us most. She is very confrontational.'

Tell me about it, Neve thought. 'I'm sure it's only temporary.'

'And her grades have slipped.'

'She's had a tough time. She was very close to her father.'

'I know she was. It is sad for you both,' the older woman continued.

Neve was horrified when without warning her lower lip started to quiver dramatically—so much for projecting calm maturity!

The genuine kindness in the other woman's voice had pricked the hard protective shell she had developed and done what all the sneers, sniggers and tabloid cameras had failed to do.

She took the tissue from the box pushed her way and blew her nose loudly.

'Thanks,' she said, not meaning the tissue.

Kindness was not something that she had been on the receiving end of much, actually not at all, once the tabloids had portrayed her as a cold-hearted, manipulative, gold-digging bitch who had married a wealthy dying man for his money. The scarlet widow, they had labelled her. It could have been worse, her brother Charlie had joked at the time—they could, he pointed out, have called her ginger.

Initially there had been a few people inclined to give her the benefit of the doubt, but they had faded away after an enterprising journalist had dug deeper and found out about the money Charlie had embezzled from James's firm.

Neve had not tried to defend herself. How could she? The fact was she *had* married a dying man who had left her pots of money and Charlie *had* embezzled a small fortune.

Nobody wanted to know she had not touched the money or that she'd agreed to James's proposal as a way of finally repaying the incredible kindness he'd shown both her and Charlie.

'And we have all made allowances for Hannah, but there is a limit. A child needs boundaries to feel safe.'

Neve accepted the not-so-subtle reprimand and gave a guilty nod, thinking boundaries only worked if the child involved listened to a word you said. If she had half the natural authority that this woman projected there wouldn't be a problem.

'I have the impression that Hannah views this new suspension before the holidays as a joke. May I make a suggestion?'

'Of course.'

'She will be spending the holidays skiing with the Palmer girl and her family?'

Neve nodded cautiously, because she was pretty sure she knew where the older woman was going with this and it would not make her life any easier.

It hadn't. Her stepdaughter's response to news that she was to spend the holiday at home with Neve and not in a fashionable ski resort with her friends had gone down pretty much the way Neve had anticipated—namely there had been shouting, abuse and finally sulky, sullen silence.

She had become enemy number one—so no change there—and the cause of every bad thing that had ever happened in her stepdaughter's life, responsible for everything, it seemed, including the weather.

She had to be doing something wrong. It wasn't meant to be this difficult, was it? Neve wondered wearily.

What had James said?

At twenty-three you haven't forgotten what it's like to be a teenager.

Well, she hadn't, but she had never been a teenager like Hannah.

I'm not asking you to be her mother, Neve. Be her friend. She'll need one.

Need maybe, but not want! Not sharing James's optimism, she hadn't really expected Hannah to look on her as a best friend, but she hadn't anticipated being the unwavering focus of all that youthful frustration and simmering hatred.

It was grueling, exhausting, and deeply depressing.

She thought things might not have been so bad if it hadn't been for the generous provision James had made for her in the will. She knew he was only trying to be kind, but that kindness had backfired big time even before the press got hold of the story.

Hannah had already considered her young stepmother a gold-digger, and the money had merely confirmed her suspicions.

Neve felt like a total failure. James had trusted her, God knew why. The truth was she wasn't qualified to look after a puppy, let alone an adolescent girl, and goodness knew what had made her agree to this in the first place.

'*Worried*? I'm not worried, I'm bored. *With you*,' Hannah added just in case Neve had not got the message.

It would have been hard not to. It was becoming clear to Neve that the cheek-turning she had been doing was not working, but the tough love alternative wasn't exactly proving to be a massive success either. There had to be some middle ground of parenting...*didn't there*?

'I've got some things planned for your break. I thought we could go shopping, and maybe if you like we could—'

The teenager cut across her. 'Thanks, but I'm not into charity shops,' she drawled, rolling her eyes. 'You do know that shocking pink clashes with ginger hair.' She gave a visible shudder as her contemptuous glance moved from Neve's sweater to her unruly auburn curls.

Neve, who owned a shop selling vintage clothes—the sweater, which she had loved on sight, had never made it to the shelves—refused to take offence. The criticism was to some extent valid: before her marriage she had shopped in charity shops, developing what kinder friends called an individual style and the less kind called weird.

Her style had not changed even after her finances had. James had given her credit cards and a very generous allowance, but she had always felt uneasy accepting his generosity. It wasn't as if they had had marriage in anything but name.

'Vintage is very in, haven't you heard?' Her customers had—business was thriving.

'*That* was never in.'

Encouraged by the grin Hannah visibly fought as she looked at the sweater in question, Neve smiled and suggested, 'You could always show me what I should be wearing?'

'Look, there's no one here to see your saintly act so why don't you just drop it, Neve? It's not as if you're fooling anyone anyway. Everyone knows why you married Dad.'

'I was very fond of your father, Hannah,' Neve said quietly.

'Fond of his money, you mean,' the youngster hit back. 'Or are you trying to tell me you'd have married him for love?'

Neve's eyes dropped guiltily. 'Your dad was a lovely man.'

'And you are a gold-digging bitch!'

This last observation was made loudly enough for the people at the next table to hear it. While her stepdaughter stormed off, she sat wishing the floor would open up and swallow her.

When it became clear that nothing short of a miracle was going to get him to his meeting on time Severo was irritated but philosophical. The very real possibility he would be forced to spend the night in his four-wheel drive was not a pleasant one, but to his mind it constituted inconvenience rather than disaster.

He rounded a bend and swore softly under his breath as he just managed to stop before he collided with the car that was slewed half across the road. Dark head bowed against the driving snow, he got out to check out the abandoned vehicle. The fact the car was locked made it seem likely that the occupants had escaped relatively unscathed.

Continuing in these weather conditions was clearly no longer a viable option. According to the last news bulletin he had heard half of the West Country was snowed in and the police were appealing to motorists to make only urgent journeys.

Stay at home, they urged. You had to get there first, he mused as he tramped back to his own vehicle. He had almost reached it when he spotted the lights in the distance. It took him another ten minutes of painful progress before he reached them.

From the look of the snow-covered vehicles in the car park of the roadside inn he had not been the only snow-bound traveller that had chanced upon this sanctuary in the middle of the bleak moor.

He was reaching for the door when his phone rang. He glanced at the caller ID and was tempted not to respond; the last time his stepmother had contacted him she had just been arrested for shoplifting.

The time before when he hadn't picked up she had raised the money she had wanted him to supply by selling off a piece of family jewellery that wasn't hers to sell, and buying it back discreetly had been time consuming.

His stepmother was time consuming, but it was dangerous to ignore her.

When he'd been young and Livia had been making a fool of his father while doing her best to turn him against his son, Severo had comforted himself with thoughts of the revenge he would one day be in a position to exact.

Now he *was* in that position, but Severo's priorities had changed. His father was in a place where his gold-digging wife could no longer hurt him, and the only power the woman who had once made his life hell wielded was to embarrass him. Actually not him—more the family.

When it came to embarrassment Severo was pretty much bomb-proof these days. As for pride in an old name, he took the view that less pride, less romanticising on past triumphs, and less being worried about getting their aristocratic hands dirty and the fortunes of the Constanza family would not have been so sadly depleted when he had been passed the mantle of power by his father.

The truth was Severo had simply lost his appetite for revenge. Not because he'd forgiven his stepmother or even that he had grown to pity her—and Livia Larsen, one-time IT girl and society hostess, had become an object of some people's pity.

Why waste time and energy when Livia was doing a pretty good job of messing up her own life without any help from him? All Severo wanted these days was for her to stay long enough in one of the expensive clinics she frequently booked herself into to actually clean up her act.

'Livia.'

He held the phone a little way from his ear, wincing at the sound of his stepmother's shrill voice berating him for his lack of feeling.

'How am I expected to live on the pittance you give me?' she demanded. 'You have more money than you need!' she complained. 'Everyone knows you're disgustingly rich. Everything you touch turns to gold.'

Severo rubbed his hand across his eyes—they felt gritty with exhaustion—and continued to listen with half an ear. It was a familiar tirade and one that did not alter no matter how much money he gave Livia, but what was the alternative?

Livia's voice became a coaxing whine. 'Just a loan?'

Severo sighed. There had been many loans and he had no doubt there would be many more.

'I'll pay you back—with interest. I know it's what your father would have wanted. Your father would have—' Her voice was drowned out by loud static before the line went dead.

He slid the phone back into his pocket, not feeling unhappy that the signal had been lost.

He was approaching the entrance to the inn when a small

figure exploded from the double doors, barrelling straight into him. Coatless and hatless and seemingly oblivious to the arctic blast of air howling down from the surrounding hills, the slim jean-clad female wearing a bright pink sweater covered with yellow daisies righted herself before running past him, then stopped and turned.

'Did you see her?'

Her eyes were wide, anxious and blue—very blue. So blue, in fact, that for a split second he registered nothing but the colour and then the moment and the opportunity to respond was gone. She was belting on and past him out into the snowy car park.

Her figure stood out, a dark blur in the swirl of white, still managing to emanate high-voltage anxiety across the space that separated them. Through the howl of the wind he heard her dismayed exclamation at the sight of a car pulling out onto the road.

'Oh, God, no!'

Severo was not a man who felt impelled to ride to the rescue of maidens in distress—such actions were open to misinterpretation and it was his experience that distress could be easily and often artistically feigned. Yet he found himself responding, albeit with reluctance, to some dormant protective instinct.

He was still a few feet from the flame-haired figure when her slumped shoulders straightened and she jumped into one of the parked vehicles and pulled away at a reckless speed. There was a time lag of several seconds before Severo realised that the lights receding into the distance belonged to his own car.

He had not only left the keys in the ignition and a laptop containing extremely sensitive information on the passenger seat, he had stood there and watched while someone stole his car, oblivious to everything except the brilliance of a pair of electric-blue eyes and a desire to offer his assistance.

He closed his eyes, called himself several rude names, not having any cathartic effect, then took a deep breath and strode into the inn.

CHAPTER TWO

THERE was a lull in the buzz of conversation and laughter inside the crowded bar as the door was flung open. The lull lengthened into a silence as people absorbed the details of the new arrival's appearance.

Tall enough to be obliged to duck his head to avoid collision with the top of the doorjamb, the dark-haired figure who stood framed in the doorway appeared utterly oblivious to the stares directed his way.

Most of his fellow stranded travellers had arrived at this sanctuary feeling to varying degrees stressed and dishevelled. This man did not look stressed, he looked irritated, and, as for dishevelled, he looked like a walking advertisement for what a glossy magazine might suggest a well-heeled, fashion-conscious business executive—always supposing he had a profile like a Greek god and a body like an Olympic rower—should aspire to achieve.

The only clue to the blizzard conditions he had just driven through was the sprinkling of rapidly melting snow on his dark mohair overcoat, open at the neck to reveal the white collar of a pristine shirt and a perfectly knotted silk tie, and the slightly wind-ruffled quality to his well-cut hair that was jet black, had outgrown a crop and was beginning to curl into his neck.

His deep-set dark eyes, fringed by long curling lashes set beneath dark well-defined brows, swept the room before they narrowed as he headed for the bar and the man who stood behind it.

The hum of conversation began once more as people melted away automatically to clear his path.

Severo got straight to the point. 'My four-wheel drive has been stolen from your car park by a woman—a redhead.'

'Well, she won't get far, will she?'

A man who sat nursing a pint piped up with a cheery, 'As far as the nearest ditch, I would think.'

Severo shook his head to dispel the unbidden slow-motion image complete with sound effects of the redhead hitting his windscreen—had she belted herself in?—and flashed a cold look at the wit sitting at the bar. The man quickly lowered his gaze into his pint glass.

'Not a lot we can do, I'm afraid,' the landlord said, still projecting what in the circumstances seemed to Severo a quite inappropriate level of optimistic cheer. 'Was there anything valuable in the car?'

Severo shook his head in a negative motion even as he listed his possessions still sitting on the passenger seat: passport, credit cards and all that information on the proposed takeover that several rivals would consider, if not priceless, certainly of extreme value.

'That's good, then.'

Severo, the strong, sculpted lines of his angular face taut with annoyance, ran a hand across the fresh stubble on his jaw before pressing a finger to the small permanent groove above his aquiline nose. He refused the drink offered by the man behind the bar and rotated his head to alleviate the knots of tension in his neck.

'You say she's a redhead?'

Severo nodded, an image of the snow-dappled copper tresses flashing into his head.

'Someone might know her but, as you can see, we've had a lot of people in...' He banged a tankard on the bar and raised his voice above the loud hum of conversation in the crowded room. 'Did anyone notice a redhead?'

It was no surprise to Severo that a number of men indicated they had—the car thief had not been the sort of woman to pass unnoticed by men—but no one, it seemed, knew who she was.

The landlord continued to be sympathetic but philosophical. 'We can't offer you a bed, but there's a fire and blankets and a well-stocked larder and bar.'

Severo, who did not share the landlord's laid-back attitude, shook his head when his host produced a bottle of malt and added, 'Like Jack here said, she can't have got far.'

Severo was seeing an image of a still body hunched lifeless over a steering wheel, snow drifting in through a smashed windscreen.

It was not his responsibility if the crazy woman had already written off his car and probably herself. He had not asked her to steal his car!

'Tomorrow when the roads clear you can—'

That might be too late. 'We should inform the authorities.'

The landlord watched as Severo fished out his phone, only to grimace at the lack of reception.

'Before you ask, the landlines are down too, have been all morning, and all the mobile signals have crashed. Have a drink. There's nothing you can do now,' he advised comfortably.

Severo accepted a coffee and considered his options. There were always options.

'Those skis I saw in the porch—who do they belong to?'

The landlord pointed out a group of young men at the far end of the room. 'Students on their way up to Aviemore,' he added by way of explanation.

Some bright spark suggested putting together a ski posse. The suggestion was made jokingly but it fed the embryo of an idea in Severo's head.

Fifteen minutes later, having resisted the well-meaning attempts to dissuade him from his course of action, Severo was strapping on a pair of borrowed skis. The borrowed ski gear was a slightly snugger fit than he would have liked, but more than adequate.

The snow still fell from rapidly darkening skies, but the wind had dropped and he made quite good time down the road, following it in the direction he had seen his car vanish.

He might have missed the abandoned vehicle had he not paused at the top of the incline to scan the horizon; if he had not he would undoubtedly have missed the light.

Changing direction, he followed the eerie beam to its source: the headlights, or at least the one not buried in the snowdrift, of his own off-roader, which was well and truly off road now!

It was the scene lifted direct from his imagination minus, thankfully, the lifeless body slumped over the wheel. The door was open but the thief had already gone, proving that she was as criminally stupid and suicidal as she had appeared; anyone with half an ounce of sense would have stayed with the vehicle and the shelter it afforded.

His belongings were still where he had left them. The sensible thing would be to gather them and make his way back to the inn. An insane woman was not his responsibility. It would serve her right if she did end up a statistic of the freak weather conditions—and he'd end up beating himself up because he could have saved her, or killed himself trying.

After a brief internal struggle he sighed. It would do his reputation no good at all if people suspected he had a conscience.

He permitted himself a grim smile when, after a quick reconnoitre of the immediate area, he discovered the imprint of footsteps that the falling snow was already beginning to cover—his thief was not far ahead.

It was not difficult to follow the footsteps. The thief, who appeared to have stumbled several times, was apparently walking in a series of ever-decreasing circles.

All sounds were muffled in the white landscape except the hoarse rasp of her own laboured respirations as she forced herself onwards. Neve's reserves of energy were totally depleted; it was sheer desperation now that drove her on. The dread lodged in her chest felt like a stone; total panic was a heavy heartbeat away.

'I like snow,' she reminded herself, panting as she added, 'I love snow.' Before falling flat on her face for the fifth time—she was counting.

If she ever had grandchildren she was going to bore them silly with this story, though stories that began with the day Granny stole a car might not be setting the best example!

She lay there and closed her eyes; she would just rest for a moment. Then she would get up because if she didn't there wouldn't be any grandchildren to set a bad example to.

She would get up because James had trusted her and she couldn't let him down.

She lay there hearing his voice.

'I have a favour to ask you, Neve.'

'Anything,' she had replied, meaning it.

James Macleod had been at college with her dad and because of that he'd given Charlie a job. Her brother had then proceeded to repay the kindness by embezzling from clients' accounts to pay for his gambling habit.

Knowing he was about to be found out, Charlie, planning to flee the country, had confessed all to Neve. She had gone to James and begged him not to bring in the police.

Amazingly he hadn't. Instead James had covered the theft using his own money, with the one proviso that Charlie seek help for his gambling addiction.

As far as Neve was concerned she was not about to refuse any favour James asked of her.

'Marry me.'

Any favour but that one.

'I've shocked you.'

'No, no,' she lied, closing her mouth. Nothing in the way James had treated her had led her to think he thought of her *that* way.

She certainly had never considered him in a romantic light. She wondered uneasily if anything she had done or said had made him think…? Blushing madly, she fumbled for a tactful way of responding without hurting his feelings.

'That's very nice of you, but it's just…I—'

'You don't love me—of course you don't. I'm old enough to be your father—'

'It's not that, it's—'

'But this wouldn't be permanent, Neve. Yes, I know that sounds strange, but bear with me, don't say anything yet, just let me explain. You see, *it's* back,' he revealed.

Neve knew the *'it'* James referred to was the disease he had been battling for years.

'And this time the prognosis is not good. I have two months tops. Don't cry, Neve, I've had time to come to terms with it and, to be honest, I'm pretty tired. My only regret is leaving Hannah.

'She will be alone and vulnerable, the target of unscrupulous people more interested in her money than her welfare. She will be a very rich young woman, Neve. If you and I marry on paper, and you adopt Hannah, become her legal guardian, nobody will be able to dispute your legality when I am gone. I can trust you. I know you will protect her.'

The tears began to seep from beneath Neve's closed eyelids. 'And a great job I'm doing of that!' she mumbled bitterly into the snow. She hit the powdery white surface with her closed fist and hissed, 'Come on, Neve, you're being pathetic. Stop wallowing and get up.'

Teeth gritted, she fought the growing compulsion to just close her eyes. She rolled onto her back; the effort exhausted her. It was while she was lying there gathering her strength that she heard the noise—yes, it was a noise, not the wind. Someone was shouting.

'Here!' she croaked. 'I'm here!'

Energising relief rushing through her body, she struggled to pull herself into a sitting position before drawing herself up onto her knees. Then, hand held above her eyes to shade them from the falling snow, she directed her hopeful gaze at the shadow emerging through the snow. *'Hannah?'*

She felt a stab of disappointment. The figure outlined against the sky was not a girl, but a man, an extremely tall man on skis. A man who, from the speed he was approaching, appeared to know what he was doing.

Not Hannah, she thought, refusing to be disheartened, but someone who could help her find Hannah.

For a horrid split second she thought the figure on skis hadn't actually seen her—he hadn't changed direction. Her heart sank, and panic set in as she imagined him passing by. She began to shout and wave her hands, but her words were whipped away by a sudden strong gust of wind. Then just as she was sure he was going to vanish he veered and came to a stop that sent a puff of fresh snow into the air a few feet away from her.

Almost sobbing with relief now, she waved at him and opened her mouth to call a warning that the ground fell away steeply, and closed it again. He was unclipping his skis and walking the last few feet. Unlike her he was not sliding and stumbling, but moving instead with an almost panther-like grace. The figure clad from head to toe in black approached.

Neve willed him to hurry. She was impatient to explain the situation and renew her search for Hannah.

'I can't tell you how glad I am to see you.'

He stood there for a moment. He might have been happy to see her too, or surprised or any number of things, but it was impossible to tell because his face was covered by a black ski mask. All she could see was the gleam of his eyes through the slits of the mask.

Without saying a word he extended a gloved hand and she took it, her eyes widening as she registered the steely strength of the man who dragged her to her feet.

'Thank you so much.' She tilted her head back to look her rescuer in the face. She had to tilt a long way; he was seriously tall. The overall effect of the mask and the all-black outfit was sinister, but, she was willing to admit, practical.

Her own face was numb but she was sure it was going to sting like crazy when the circulation returned to it and her frozen extremities.

'Have you seen anyone else? A girl about fourteen?'

He didn't respond to her anxious query, just carried on staring down at her.

'Dark hair, she's wearing a red duffel coat.' A warm colour but the coat wasn't—it was thin and not waterproof. She caught her wobbling lower lip between her teeth and said with determined optimism, 'Which will be useful—we'll be able to spot her miles away.'

Her tone invited him to come back with something appropriately upbeat, but when all he did was carry on staring at her with the same unnerving intensity, Neve gave him a gentle nudge.

'I mean, red stands out for miles, ask any ginger person.' She tried, but Neve couldn't force the laugh past her tight, aching throat muscles. 'We will find her, won't we?'

'Find who?' His narrowed eyes scanned her face. The freckles across her nose stood out in the ghostly pallor that was alleviated by the patches of colour where the driving snow had chafed the soft skin of her cheeks to a painful pink. More worrying was the bluish tinge of her lips, a warning sign he might have noticed a precious minute earlier if he had not been transfixed by the brilliance of electric-blue eyes. In his defence they were extraordinary.

'Who?' Had he been listening to a word she'd said? 'Hannah, of course.'

He unzipped his jacket and draped it around her narrow shoulder. 'She's a redhead too?'

'No, red *coat*.' The heat embedded in the padded fabric was tempting, but as much as she appreciated the gesture she couldn't let him. 'That's really kind of you, but I can't allow you—'

'Allow implies I asked permission.'

The irritation in his deep voice was echoed in the dark eyes that meshed briefly with her own.

'I didn't.'

'But you'll get cold...'

Ignoring her protest, he took her right wrist.

She was too surprised to resist as he threaded it into the sleeve as if she were a child and then took her left hand and did the same.

'But— Ooh!' He drew the two sides of the jacket together so forcibly he almost jerked her off her feet. Teeth chattering violently, she looked up at him. His dark eyes glittered back at her through the slits in the mask, projecting a level of anger that was bewildering.

'I really don't need your—'

Severo swore and grabbed her by the shoulders. This was no time for tact and diplomacy. He studied her upturned features with a baffled expression. She couldn't take his jacket, but this was the same woman who had taken his car without a second thought?

What she *needed*, in his opinion, was therapy, and so did he for being out here.

He pulled the zip all the way up until just her small tip-tilted nose peeped out over the top.

'I'd love to chat with you, but we have no time for a debate. Also, for the record, I am not being chivalrous, this is purely practical. I'm wearing layers.' And even through them the bite of the cold went bone deep.

The chill went deeper still when he thought of what sort of condition she would have been in if he had not found her when he had. How long would she have lasted—another hour… less?

He felt his anger surge. She seemed utterly oblivious to the danger she was in.

'You are dressed for a stroll along a beach.' The harsh condemnation in his voice made Neve take an involuntary step backwards. 'It is people like you,' he continued, warming to the theme, 'people who have no respect for nature and the elements, who wander into the mountains ill equipped and expect other people to risk their lives to save them for their foolishness.' He shook his head and searched the pale face tilted up to him; it felt like yelling at a kitten. 'You've no idea what I'm talking about, have you?'

'I've never tried to climb a mountain.'

He released a hissing sound of irritation and said, 'The subject is closed. We are wasting time.'

'You're right.' Neve was relieved he understood the urgency of the situation. 'I was thinking if we found some high ground—'

What school of survival had she attended? 'We need shelter, not high ground.'

'No, that won't work, we need to see—'

Sounding annoyed at the interruption, he cut across her. 'See what exactly?'

'Hannah,' she said, finally placing the accent that had intrigued her since he began to speak: Italian.

There had been several Italian waiters in the restaurant they had stopped at for lunch. It would be a coincidence if he had been one of them. Though now that she thought about it, she did not remember any of them being this tall.

He shook his head. *'Hannah?'*

'I was heading towards...' she made a vague gesture behind her with her hand '...That way and she was just in front of me in a blue—' Neve shook head crazily; she couldn't recall the make of her own car '—car. Which way did you come? Did you see her?' He shook his head and turned away, scanning the horizon, sizing up the most direct route back to the road.

Neve caught his sleeve and tugged hard. He turned his head, his glance drifting from the fingers curled into the fabric of his sweater to the tumble of wild copper-gold curls around the heart-shaped face turned up to his.

'But you *must* have. Were you on the road?'

'I saw no one.' Severo struggled to contain his escalating impatience. 'We are not equipped to undertake a rescue operation.' Bit late in the day to realise this, and for all he knew this Hannah might be a figment of this woman's imagination. If not he hoped she had already found safety, but the brutal truth was if she hadn't adding to the casualty list with their own lives was not going to help. 'This woman, if she exists, will have to take care of herself.'

'She's not a woman, she's a child! What do you mean *if*? We have to—'

'We?'

Neve grimaced as she realised she had been presuming he would be willing to help her. Clearly she had been wrong; she didn't usually judge, but it was hard not to feel contemptuous of someone who looked after number one.

She began to unzip the jacket.

'Fine, I'll find her myself. But when you're able, could you inform the authorities that a fourteen-year-old is missing? If that's not too much bother?'

As it was nobody even knew Hannah was out there somewhere. 'And that's my fault too, for not thinking,' she mumbled as she tried to shrug off his jacket.

Severo swore under his breath and, leaning down, pulled the two sides of the jacket together. 'You can tell them yourself when we get back to civilization,' he said as he pulled the zip all the way up to her chin again.

Neve zipped it down far enough to speak. 'No you don't understand. I can't go back. I have to find Hannah. She was—'

'No, *you* don't understand.' The woman had the survival instincts of a lemming.

'Hannah—'

Severo gritted his teeth and tightened his grip on her shoulder as she struggled desperately to pull free. 'What we have to do is find shelter.' It would not be as easy as it sounded; in the last few minutes the snow had begun to fall heavier than ever.

Severo lifted his narrowed eyes to the leaden sky. Another half-hour and the light would be gone. Their best bet, he reasoned, was to head back to the abandoned off-roader. That would provide at least some shelter from the elements. Even retracing his footsteps in this near white-out was not, he recognized, going to be easy in the unfamiliar terrain. He had a good sense of direction, but in these conditions it would be all too easy to become fatally disorientated.

'No…no!' Neve panted, struggling wildly but with little effect against the steely restraint of his grasp. 'You don't understand, I have to—'

Severo, his voice harsh with impatience, cut across her shrill impassioned plea. 'You may have a death wish, but I do not.'

Neve regarded him with contempt and set her jaw. 'Fine, you go back or wherever, but I'm going on.'

Severo watched her lips, seeing them move, tuning out the hysterical babble, but unable, even at a moment when all his attention needed to be concentrated on the crucial matter of survival, not to appreciate the lushness of the pink outline.

Under the ski mask a fleeting grimace twisted his wide sensual mouth. As he acknowledged the male weakness a moment later it was replaced by an expression of steely resolve. Time was of the essence; to be out here when darkness fell was not a good idea.

'What are you—?' Neve let out a startled yelp as she found herself heaved casually off the ground a moment later and slung over a male shoulder. 'Put me down!' she shrieked.

He grunted in response to the kick she landed, but did not reply to her demand. He just carried on walking, head bent against the driving snow.

CHAPTER THREE

SEVERO placed his burden down on her feet.

He shot out a steadying hand when her knees sagged. 'You are all right?'

He sounded more irritated than concerned, and Neve weakly batted his gloved hand away. *All right?* Just her luck to get rescued—or was it kidnapped?—by a man of few words and all of them stupid!

'No, I'm *not* all right!' she panted.

She had been hauled cross country against her will with all the dignity of a sack of coal, she was exhausted, she was cold, she was paralysed with fear and guilt every time she thought of Hannah!

All right?

She bit her quivering lip, resisting the strong temptation to lie face down in the snow and cry. She took a deep sustaining breath and reminded herself she was not a wimp—she just had wimpish tendencies.

Severo took her reply at face value and chose not to notice the quivering resentment in her voice. He flexed his shoulders, aware that she was struggling not to fall apart; nine out of ten people already would have. The redhead might be stupid but she was also gutsy.

'Well, you're alive.' Alive was something she might not be if he had not found her. Severo felt his anger mount as he considered her criminal stupidity. 'So stop moaning.'

The terse direction made her blink.

'I don't know who you think you are—' She stopped, realising that she didn't have the faintest idea who he was or what he was except selfish, insensitive and extremely fit. The latter was a given—after the fifteen-minute slog through the snow carrying her he had to be exhausted, but there was nothing to suggest even slight fatigue in his manner. Her glance slid to his broad chest; he was not even breathing hard under the black fleece.

'Just who are you anyway?'

'I'm the man who saved your life. You can,' he added sardonically, 'thank me later, when I will happily give you my life history.'

'A name would be quite sufficient, and I didn't ask to be saved.' Neve knew that she sounded quite unbelievably childish and ungrateful, but her frustration at being forcibly brought here when she ought to be searching for Hannah made it hard for her to be gracious. 'I didn't *need* saving.'

His lips twisted into an ironic smile as he fished out his mobile and tried for a signal: nothing. 'Yeah, I could see that you had the situation under control.'

Neve, who had held her breath while he tried his phone, watched him slide it back into his pocket, barely registering his sarcasm.

'No signal?'

He shook his head.

Neve pulled her spirits out of the depressing downward spiral they had taken since Hannah had run out of the inn, and straightened her shoulders. This was not the time to get negative. Looking around, she finally took in the lit building behind her. Lights meant people, and this place was lit up like a Christmas tree.

'What is this place?' Other than the answer to her prayers. The people inside would be able to raise the alarm, finally. Of course, the search parties would already be out if she had thought before acting, and Hannah might already be safe, not out there somewhere, lost, cold... Neve shook her head, refusing to follow the thought to its horrid conclusion.

Stay positive.

She would find Hannah, and her stepdaughter would be all right.

She had to be all right!

Severo watched with growing fascination as the flicker of expressions moved across her pale face. In a matter of seconds he registered a gamut of emotions, all extreme, from deep despair to steely-eyed determination.

Born in another age she would have made a great silent-screen actress—that face could convey more than several pages of dialogue.

When he didn't respond Neve brushed a wet strand of hair from her cheek and angled a questioning look up at him.

'A barn conversion, I'd say, and a safe haven.' He was beginning to wonder if this woman had at any point had the faintest idea of how much danger she had been in. Her attitude certainly made it seem unlikely.

Lucky for her she led a charmed life and he had developed a fascination for red hair and electric-blue eyes.

Neve took a deep breath. She didn't want a safe haven while Hannah was still out there. 'Hopefully the people here will not be too worried about their own skins, unlike some, and—'

Without turning, he cut her off. He did not need to be hailed a hero—in fact he would have run a mile to avoid such a scenario—but a simple thank-you might be nice.

'Can you save the reading of my character until we get out of this? We *cowards* do not have conversations in the middle of a blizzard—and don't try to run because I will find the necessity to catch you irritating.'

In the act of turning, Neve froze. 'Is that a threat?' she

demanded through teeth that were now chattering from a combination of cold and shock.

'It is an understatement,' he corrected, throwing the comment over his shoulder as he negotiated the snow-covered flight of steps.

Light streamed from the glass panel that led down to the big entrance door, and the slits cut deep into the blocks of stone, but it was the apex wall that appeared to be formed totally of glass panels that had made the place visible from the other side of the valley.

Severo banged on the door. When there was no reply he alternated banging and then ringing the bell. He made enough noise to rouse the dead but nobody inside stirred—were they deaf, or possibly just cautious of strangers appearing from nowhere?

The question was academic. If he was terrifying someone he would make his apologies. He did not need a thermometer to tell him that the temperature was dropping. Right now his main priority was getting inside before things got serious.

How much more serious do you want, asked the voice in his head, stuck in the middle of a blizzard with some felonious madwoman?

To look at her standing there in the jacket that reached her knees she looked cute and fragile, the sort of woman that aroused protective instincts in men—the ones who had not been kicked by her, at any rate.

He was not one of them. She had landed a couple of hefty kicks before she had quietened down, which would have caused a lot more damage had her footwear not been woefully inadequate for the conditions.

'Stay there!' He flung the terse instruction over his shoulder before working his way around the side of the building. He almost missed the side entrance, a glass-panelled door that was half obscured by a drift that had formed up against the side of the building.

A quick survey revealed it did not look nearly as substantial as the oak-panelled main door. His luck was turning, and not before time. All he had to do now was get to it, which required shifting the several feet of snow that blocked it.

Using his gloved hands, Severo began to clear a path to the door, building up a steady rhythm as he made a narrow slippery corridor through the snow.

'I said not to move.'

It was spooky. He had not even turned around. The man clearly had eyes in the back of his head.

His manner suggested he was not accustomed to people ignoring his instructions. 'Yes, you did,' she agreed, unable to repress a sharp intake of breath as she plunged her hands into the snow.

He stopped shovelling and turned his head. 'What do you think you're doing?' Other than shaking so hard he could hear her teeth rattle from feet away.

Neve exhaled a gusty breath that froze white in the air between them. Through the fog she could see the glittering slits of his eyes and ice crystals on the lashes that fringed them.

The man had the most ludicrously long eyelashes. Irritated she was storing such irrelevant information, she brushed the snow from her own eyes and retorted, 'Helping.' Aware this claim was something of an exaggeration—this wasn't nearly as easy as he had made it look—she was unable to keep the defensive note from her voice.

Severo expelled an irritated sigh through clenched teeth. At least she had followed him and not run in the opposite direction. He bent across to where she knelt and pulled her small hands from the snow. Her fine-boned wrists were incredibly narrow and her slender fingers were not just tinged with blue, they *were* blue.

Their glances locked, and he thought, Not as blue as her incredible eyes—but then nothing he had ever seen was.

Clicking his tongue with exasperation that was partly reserved for his continued fascination with her cornflower-blue
stare, he hauled her to her feet and pulled the sleeves of his
borrowed jacket over her freezing extremities before returning
to his task with renewed energy. A frozen felon on his hands
would be bound to mean a lot of questions.

'I am perfectly capable of—' A sudden lull in the wind
meant that her words emerged as a forceful yell.

He placed a gloved hand to her lips. 'I have witnessed your
capabilities.' Unlike her, he had adjusted the volume. This did
not make his delivery any less forceful, but it did reveal an
attractive gravelly rasp in his deep accented voice.

'I was only trying to help.' Most people would have been
grateful, but this man was clearly not a team player.

'It will not be *helpful* if you get frostbite.'

Her rescuer had a point, Neve conceded, aware that she had
lost all feeling in her fingers. Had Hannah been wearing her
gloves? A mental image of her stepdaughter, a small figure
at the mercy of the elements, flashed before her eyes, and the
fear rose like bile in her throat.

She took a deep breath and fought down the panic. 'What
shall I do?' If he wanted to be in charge, fine, she could live
with that, but she couldn't stand there and do nothing now.

He flashed her a look over his shoulder. 'I think nothing
would be safest.'

Nasty sarcastic rat, Neve thought, watching as he rapidly
completed his task. She did not have to wait for long—it took
him another two minutes to access the door.

He gave a satisfied grunt and looked around for a suitable
blunt object; unlike the large panelled areas in the front of the
building, this glass panel was not of the same impregnable
quality.

Severo quickly found a suitable smooth stone. 'Turn around
and cover your face.'

Her eyes widened as she realised his intentions. 'You're going to break in?'

His hand lowered. 'A nice touch of moral outrage, but a tad, shall we say, hypocritical?'

The cryptic comment sailed over Neve's head; the thought of being party to breaking and entering made her deeply uneasy.

'Couldn't you try knocking again?' she suggested, forcing the words past her chattering teeth.

'Or we could go away and come back tomorrow?' he said sardonically.

Neve loosed a cry of alarm as he raised his arm again. She covered her face with her hands, watching through parted fingers as his hand moved in a smooth arc towards the glass panel in the door.

She had tensed in anticipation of the sound of smashing glass when he stopped just short of impact and, as she watched, tried the door handle.

The door swung inwards and she heard him laugh; it was not an unattractive sound.

Grinning to himself behind his mask, Severo dropped the stone and stepped inside, trying not to bring in any more of the small avalanche of snow that had fallen inwards when he'd opened the door—it was already beginning to melt on the surface of the black and white chequered floor tiles.

Unlike the rest of the house, this room was in darkness, though not *really* dark—the light from the snow reflected off the pale shiny surfaces. It appeared to be a laundry room of sorts, with stainless-steel work surfaces above white storage units; a power switch glowed red on the panel on a washing machine but it stood silent.

Stamping his feet on the tiled floor to knock the snow from his boots, he reached for the light switch, blinking when the room was flooded with harsh light. The small figure swamped in the borrowed ski jacket stood framed in the doorway.

'Are you coming in or what?'

The choice being to freeze to death or accept the invitation, Neve stepped inside wishing she could be as totally at ease with the entire breaking and entering situation as this man appeared to be.

Maybe he'd had experience with similar situations, she speculated uneasily, but on the plus side he did seem like a person who might be useful in hazardous situations. Though she couldn't imagine, given his initial reaction, that he'd think it a good idea to go back out there and search for Hannah, it was possible he'd warm to the idea more if she offered to pay him.

Well, with or without his help she was going back out. Once I've thawed out a little, she thought, rubbing her numb fingers together. She didn't need him.

You carry on telling yourself that, Neve.

Ignoring the voice in her head, she glanced towards the sinister figure of her rescuer.

Outside in the harsh and unforgiving landscape, although she had been unwilling to admit it, his undeniable physical presence and strength had been comforting. Inside the confines of the room they were almost oppressive. Even if the face that was hidden behind the mask was pleasant or plain, with a body like his he was never going to fade into the background.

Long of limb and broad of shoulder, he looked all hard bone and lean muscle. It was as her slightly unfocused gaze drifted upwards from his feet that she became aware of his questioning posture.

'What?' she said, embarrassment making her voice accusing. Well, it was extremely embarrassing to be caught ogling a man's body even if the scrutiny was totally objective.

'I said would you close the...?' Emitting an irritated sound, he clicked his tongue and leaned in towards her.

Neve instinctively shrank back, a strangled cry escaping her lips before she realised that he was just closing the door.

His hand still resting on the wall beside the doorjamb, he swept a concerned downward glance at her upturned features.

Neve looked at her feet and heard him say, 'What's wrong?'

She shook her head, still avoiding the dark gleam of his eyes through the slits of the mask. She felt deeply embarrassed by her stupid instinctive reaction.

Her instincts were still embarrassing her.

It was bizarre. She had to make a conscious effort to put one foot in front of the other; she was unable to stop shaking, half dead with cold and, despite all that, or hopefully *because* of it, she was conscious of the weirdest *tug*.

She had this insane impulse, not to draw back, but to lean into him. She was drawn to his sheer physical presence, his strength and the warmth of the big body. The longer he stayed curved over her, projecting this testosterone force field, the more difficult it was to resist the bizarre compulsion.

'What did you think I was going to do?'

Neve shook her head mutely. He'd put his own interpretation on her silence, but what could she say? I thought you were going to kiss me.

What would it have felt like?

Appalled by the dreamy question that surfaced in her head, she gave a fractured sigh of relief when he straightened up.

Her hands, still crossed in a protective gesture over her heaving chest, fell limply to her sides. She watched through the screen of her lashes as he walked across the room.

There was something totally riveting about the way he moved.

Neve pushed the thought away and lowered her gaze to the chequered floor tiles. 'You…you startled me.'

'Relax, you are quite safe.'

The mockery in his deep voice made her squirm. 'Nice to know.'

'I admit you might scrub up well,' he said, sounding insultingly doubtful, 'but right now, *cara*, you are not, believe me, going to drive any man wild with lust.' No man in his right mind, certainly, but Severo was beginning to doubt his own mental health.

The question was not why on earth did he want to kiss the tip of her red nose, it was why on earth was he here? He valued logic; he prided himself on his judgement—what sort of judgement had made him risk life and limb in a blizzard?

Did he really think she needed him to point out her deficiencies? 'I suppose you like your women to be decorative and dumb.' It was not a question, just a fact of life.

'I can see you find my sex life fascinating, but can we leave this discussion for later?'

Struggling to maintain the illusion of dignity, she followed him through the door muttering under her breath. 'It's always nice to have something to look forward to.'

One thing that really got under his skin was the sort of woman who always had to have the last word.

CHAPTER FOUR

THE softly lit living area was open-plan, a large lofty space dominated by a wood burner at one end and a high-spec ultra-modern kitchen at the other.

Severo took in his surroundings in one sweeping glance, dismissing as he did so the 'lights being on an automatic timer to discourage burglars' explanation.

This place was definitely lived in, he decided, glancing at today's date on the newspaper spread out on a sofa.

Neve hung back in the doorway getting the lived-in vibe too. 'W…we can't just walk into someone else's home, and touch their things,' she added pointedly as he lifted the lid of a laptop.

Severo closed the lid with a snap; her sudden respect for others' property struck him as ironic. 'What do you suggest we do—press our noses to the glass while we freeze?' He flicked a sideways glance her way and thought, In your case freeze some more. Even the soft mood lighting did not disguise the fact she looked one step away from collapse.

'No, but—' She stopped and shook her head, finishing lamely, 'It doesn't feel right.'

The head shake had been a mistake. The distant buzz got a lot louder as the angles of the room began to shift and tilt in a way that made her feel queasy. She had zero experience of fainting, but she did wonder whether this might be the build-up.

He already obviously thought she was clueless, which was pretty annoying considering she had been looking after herself since she was fourteen, but Neve had no intention of reinforcing the 'helpless little woman' image by falling at his feet.

Even as she advised herself sternly to get a grip she swayed gently.

'It feels a lot *righter* than dying of exposure.'

He turned and Neve reached out to grab the back of a chair to steady herself; her fingers, still numb and uncooperative, flexed feebly and slid uselessly off the wooden bar.

'Sit.' His hands were on her shoulders.

She blinked, wondering how he had materialised at her side without her noticing as she responded to the pressure. For a big man he moved quickly and silently.

'Deep breaths,' he said. Pushing his fingers under the wet hair on her nape, he forced her head forward and between her knees.

His soothing voice and calm manner helped her recover as much as the air she dragged into her lungs. It only took a couple of moments for the buzzing to retreat and her head to clear.

Bracing herself for his reaction to her uncharacteristic girly display of weakness, Neve pushed her wet hair back from her face with both hands and straightened up. She needn't have worried—his attention was directed not at her, but on the galleried landing above.

'Do you hear someone?' she asked hopefully.

He shook his head and scanned her pale face. 'Feeling better?'

'I'm fine.'

Her response drew an irritated frown.

Neve's glance drifted hopefully towards the phone sitting on the table behind him. 'The phone?'

Severo followed the direction of her gaze and picked it up. After a moment he shook his head. 'Dead.' Not actually a major surprise, but her face fell as if she were a child whose ice cream had been snatched away.

This redhead should never play poker. The women in Severo's life rarely said what they meant, they generally chose less direct methods to get what they wanted, so to be around someone who was not only straight talking to the point of rudeness, but broadcast her every minute change of mood, had a certain novelty value.

No doubt the novelty would wear thin, the same way after repeated exposure he would not find blue eyes so startling.

'Somebody appears to have left in a hurry,' he observed, walking across to the table laid with an untouched meal. He pulled off a glove and stabbed some of the food with a finger. 'Cold,' he said, pulling off the other glove and flexing his long fingers to revive the sluggish circulation.

Neve watched as he walked to the bottom of the big curving staircase where he called out, his deep voice echoing around the vaulted room.

There was a silence.

'At least the fire is still lit,' he said, studying the thermostat dial on the wall before switching it to full blast. He glanced back to where the redhead was getting unsteadily to her feet; she looked as shaky on her legs as a new foal.

'What's your name?' he asked, tilting his head to check out the galleried landing that ran the length of the room.

'Neve. Neve Gray, no, Macleod.'

'Think about it and get back to me when you've decided.'

Neve angled a glare up at his face and gritted, 'Neve Macleod.'

'Right, Neve, I'll check out upstairs, you take off that wet stuff.'

It was not a suggestion.

The man was clearly used to issuing orders and it was revealing that he took compliance for granted; presumably there was a girlfriend or even wife somewhere who jumped when he snapped his fingers.

He returned a few moments later; in his absence Neve hadn't moved a muscle. Even had she wanted to respond to his casual order she couldn't have, but she could see no point in removing clothes when she was so cold that her bones ached with it. Besides, the action would require energy and hers had seeped away.

She stood there shivering while he paused at the bottom of the stairs to peel the ski mask from his head.

'Nobody there,' he announced. 'Though the open drawers and wardrobe suggest a hasty departure. Very *Marie Celeste*, but I do have a theory,' he offered, passing a hand back and forth across his short dark hair as he walked to the fire and swung open the glass door. Dipping into the log basket, he threw a couple onto the glowing embers.

Neve didn't ask about his theory; she barely heard what he said. She was staring transfixed by the features that had been hidden until now beneath the mask—features that were not plain and *definitely* not pleasant! Not even in the confines of her head had she ever called a man beautiful before, but he was—he was totally, jaw-droppingly perfect.

Beautiful but without being in any way pretty, raw sex appeal oozing from every perfect pore, each individual feature in his face gave new meaning to faultless perfection, from the sensual curve of his wide, sensually sculpted mouth to the arched angle of his ebony brows.

Utterly transfixed, she held her breath as her fascinated gaze slid over each amazing angle and fascinating hollow of his oval face, from the high, carved cheekbones to the aquiline nose. His deep-set eyes, the only feature previously visible, were only a shade lighter than the incredibly long ebony lashes that fringed them.

She expelled a shaky sigh as her stomach muscles quivered violently. He was big and hard and oozed both danger and an earthy raw sex appeal she had been conscious of even when his face had been concealed.

'Come to the fire—you're still shaking,' Severo observed, annoyed with himself for allowing the mystery of the deserted house to distract him from the immediate problem, which by the look of her was imminent collapse and probably hypothermia.

At the sound of his voice Neve shook her head and blinked like someone surfacing from a trance. She'd not drooled, but she had come pretty close her embarrassment was profound.

'I'm fine.'

She had never been a sucker for a pretty face and this was not the right time to discover her inner bimbo! Pull yourself together, Neve! So he's easy on the eye—it's what's underneath that counts.

Especially if what's underneath is a body as incredible as she suspected his was!

Disassociating herself from the comment in her head, Neve brought her lashes down in a protective screen, hoping that he couldn't hear the frantic thud of her heart from across the room.

His sensual lips twisted in an irritated grimace as his glance swept her face. 'Fine? Now there's a surprise—considering how rich the English language is, your vocabulary seems painfully limited.'

'I'm a bit cold.'

'*A bit cold…* I'm assuming you graduated with first-class honours in understatement. I am no expert on such matters, if you discount a year of pre-med, but I do not think that lips are meant to be blue.'

Neve lifted a shaky hand to cover her tremulous lips and stared up at him, trying to imagine him as a doctor and getting bogged down by the bedside-manner section of the job. 'I said I'm cold.'

'I am cold. You,' he decided, 'are in danger of succumbing to hypothermia. And we will get on a lot better if you spare me the incessant stoicism,' he observed, sounding bored.

'I don't want to "get on better" with you.'

Ignoring the childish retort, he lifted a hand and gestured for her to come to the fire. When she didn't respond he crossed the room and stood looking down at her for a moment before planting both hands heavily on her shoulders.

Holding her eyes, he steered her towards the glass-fronted wood burner. His sloe-dark gaze remained trained on Neve's paper-pale face as he dragged a small armchair across the slate-flagged floor.

Neve's knees folded under the pressure of the hands on her shoulders as he urged her into it.

Severo dropped into a squatting position and began to unzip the snow-coated oversized jacket. He peeled it away to reveal the bright pink sweater she wore beneath.

Neve roused herself enough to make a token protest when he began to remove the saturated sweater, but he rather predictably ignored her.

'I'm not helpless,' she protested, feeling perilously close to it. Also perilously close was his chest and quite stupidly she wanted to lay her head on it.

'*Dio mio*, woman, do you ever stop complaining?'

The sodden sweater made a squelching noise as he tossed it carelessly on the floor. Without the padding she was revealed as slim and sleek with surprisingly generous curves that were in perfect proportion to her delicate petite frame.

Her outraged blue gaze flew to his face. 'Do you ever stop issuing orders?' she countered in husky exasperation.

He flashed her a mocking grin. 'Some are born to lead, others to follow, preferably in silence.' Though her voice with the sexy little rasp was actually quite easy on the ear.

'And I suppose these born leaders in your world are all

m…male.' The words emerged through clenched teeth she couldn't seem to stop shaking.

Under the sweater she was wearing a thin cotton tee shirt that clung damply, revealing not only the outline of her spine and heaving ribcage, but the lacy pattern of her bra and the clearly defined outline of her nipples thrusting through the thin fabric.

It was the last detail that riveted Severo's attention and sent a kick of lust through his body. The more he tried not to think about a breast fitting perfectly in his hand, the more he saw it there. The more he saw his mouth moving over the smooth silky flesh, teasing…tasting.

Closing off this line of thought abruptly, which was not as easy as it should have been, he inhaled, drawing air into his lungs through flared nostrils. Along with the oxygen meant to clear his head came the scent of her skin and the light floral fragrance she used and he remained painfully aroused.

When he didn't respond Neve lifted her head. Following the direction of his stare, she let out a yelp, covered her chest with her hands and promptly felt a total fool.

'Relax, *cara*,' he said, thinking, Good advice, Severo, take it.

'I'm cold,' she said defensively.

His lashes swept downwards, brushing the dark bands of colour that highlighted the sharp chiselled angles of his cheekbones.

'I'd noticed.'

Deliberately redirecting his gaze, he snatched a woollen throw from a nearby sofa and dropped it casually in her lap.

'You have nothing I have not seen before.'

His over-the-top reaction, Severo concluded, was the result of the adrenaline still flooding his bloodstream; either that or there was something about this woman that made him regress fifteen years. It had been a long time since his libido had strained this hard at the leash of his iron control.

His amused attitude made Neve feel like a gauche teenager.

'Take the rest of your stuff off. I'll get some towels.'

Neve stared at him incredulously. Was the man serious?

'I'm not taking anything off.'

He gave a very Latin shrug and flashed a wolfish grin, not appearing to notice her non-negotiable tone. Still smiling in the same stomach-flipping way, he looked down into her heart-shaped face and shrugged.

'Fine. If you're not up to the task, I'll do it for you.'

Neve closed her mouth over the *you wouldn't dare* that leapt to her lips, recognising that such a statement might seem an invitation to a certain sort of man, and watched him bound energetically up the stairs—he was almost definitely that sort of man.

As she closed her eyes the image of his strong hands peeling off her clothes began to play in her head. It was the little kick of excitement mixed in with the horror that made her decide there was no point in taking the risk and calling his bluff.

Slowed by her cold, stiff fingers, she had clumsily managed to strip down to her bra, her wet jeans she'd managed to get halfway down her numb legs, when she heard his footsteps on the stairs.

She picked up the blanket and hastily draped the folds of tartan wool fabric around her shoulders.

She felt her chest tighten as she watched, her heart pounding, as he walked across the room towards her. He was obviously not similarly inhibited when it came to stripping.

His wet outer clothes, at least from the waist down, had been replaced. A pair of worn blue denims that were a couple of inches too short in the leg and a few more inches too wide around the waist now covered his legs. He hadn't bothered fastening the belt and they had slid down to his narrow hips, revealing his flat belly and a directional arrow of dark hair.

Neve struggled not to follow the direction it pointed in.

But there was no safe place to look because above the waist he was naked except for a towel looped around his neck. His sleek bronzed upper body had the most incredible muscle definition she had ever seen, broad shoulders, flat abdomen.

Neve tried to look anywhere but at his lean muscled torso and failed miserably, conscious of a dragging liquid sensation low in her abdomen as she stared.

She was ashamed of her helpless physical response to him but at least he appeared oblivious to her discomfort—she hoped!

Meeting her wary gaze, he placed the pile of towels he carried on a chair. His glance dropped to the jeans concertinaed around her ankles. The little beads of sweat along her upper lip suggested that she had been struggling in his absence.

Severo felt something break free inside him, something that felt suspiciously like tenderness.

'You're going to have to accept a little help, *cara*.' Without waiting for her response—it would obviously be negative; the woman took self-reliance to unattractive extremes—he dropped to his knees in front of her and, sliding his hands under the blanket, began to ease the wet, heavy denim down her legs.

Neve looked down at the dark head of the kneeling man. She didn't move, she didn't breathe—not until, having completed his task, he laid a hand against her calf. Then her control snapped and she flinched away, unable to bear the sensations crawling under her skin.

He swore. 'You're like ice.' He began to rub her bare legs vigorously with his hands, working his way up from her slender ankles, over her calves to her knees. His touch made her stomach muscles quiver violently with tension.

'Can you even feel me?'

'Not much…' she lied, thinking, *If only*, as she bit her lip and squeezed her eyes closed. Despite this she could still see the disturbing—on so many levels—image of his strong hands, the long fingers moving against her skin.

She tried to think through the swirl of conflicting emotions in her head. Why did this man affect her this way? There had to be a perfectly logical explanation for all this weirdness.

Sex-starved and desperate would have fitted the symptoms had it not been for the fact she had never had a strong sex drive. It was probably why she'd never had a real boyfriend. Resisting uncontrollable burning lust had never been a problem for her, possibly because her lust had never even ignited. When it came to sex all she had felt was mild curiosity about what she was missing, but so far she'd refused the offers of men who had been eager to show her. The idea of sex without any emotional connection just didn't work for her.

She caught her breath sharply and flinched as she felt his long brown fingers move a little higher over the bare flesh of her thigh.

He angled a questioning look at her face.

'That hurts,' she lied.

This, she told herself, was clearly some mild form of post-traumatic stress, not that it felt particularly mild or, for that matter, post anything—his touch was causing her stress to reach unprecedented levels.

'It's meant to hurt. Do not be a baby.'

Her lips tightened at this bracing advice.

'I'm trying,' he continued, his voice, it seemed to her, slightly strained as he concentrated on the task in hand, 'to get your circulation moving.'

His own circulation was very active.

'Make up your mind. I th...thought you didn't want me to be b...brave.'

'I want you—' Severo's head lifted, his eyes brushing her face as he broke off, appearing to lose his drift mid-sentence.

His fixed hypnotic stare was so intense that it had an oddly paralysing effect on Neve. She was tempted to give herself up to the enervating heat that seeped through both her body and mind as the silence stretched.

She was tempted to stop fighting.

Stop fighting what? Or who? asked the voice in her head.

'You can't count them. I've tried.' She forced the croaky words out but was unable to produce a creditable grin to accompany them.

He angled a dark brow.

'My freckles.'

Without responding to her feeble effort at humour, he reached for a towel from the stack he had fetched and continued his task, using it instead of his bare hands. This actually did hurt, but Neve found it infinitely preferable to the more disturbingly intimate skin-to-skin contact.

Still disturbing enough though. His ministrations were clinical but her reaction to them was not. She only managed to bear it for a few more uncomfortable moments before she blurted, 'Thanks, that's much better now, Mr...?' She stopped, realising she didn't even know his name.

The half-naked man had just been responsible for the most erotic experience in her life—possibly making her the saddest twenty-four-year-old on the planet—and she didn't even know his name!

He stopped, studied her face for a moment, then nodded and rose to his feet with a fluid grace that typified all his actions. 'Severo. Severo Constanza.'

Neve had never seen the appeal of the Latin male; she wished she still couldn't.

'We had lunch at an Italian restaurant today before the snow started. I don't think I saw you there?'

It took him a few seconds to realise that she was asking him if he was a waiter. Severo had been anticipating his name eliciting a reaction but not this one!

His sense of humour reasserted itself. 'No, you would not have.'

'Are you laughing at me?' she asked, suspicious of his grave expression, but relieved that some of the tension in the air appeared to have dissipated.

'No, myself. If ever I feel in danger of believing my own press releases I shall know where to come to have my ego deflated.'

Her lashes fluttered wider. 'You have press releases?'

He shrugged. 'A figure of speech.'

Still frowning suspiciously across at him, she sat in the armchair set beside the fire and tucked her legs up under her as she drew the blanket up to her chin.

'Shall I see if I can rustle up something to eat and drink?' Without waiting for her response, he moved across to the kitchen area and started opening doors.

To call the atmosphere cosy would have been a massive overstatement; a person could not feel *cosy* when they were in the same room as the human equivalent of a wolf, but the antagonism had definitely lessened and she was hungry.

Had the antagonism been replaced by something more dangerous?

The thought made Neve, in the act of relaxing into her chair, stiffen. As she rose, the blanket covering her from her neck to her feet, she did not pause to identify this dangerous *something*—anything that made her lose focus and lessened her sense of urgency was dangerous.

'I'm not hungry. I need to find Hannah.'

Severo expelled a hissing sigh through clenched teeth and dragged a frustrated hand through his dark hair as he moved to intercept her. 'Sit down before you fall down!'

Her chin went up, the angry flush of colour that washed over her fair skin condensing into bright patches of angry colour on her cheeks as she glared up at him.

'I have to find Hannah. Don't worry,' she added quickly.

'I'm not asking you to help.' Just because he looked like her personal identikit image of a hero who laughed in the face of danger. it did not mean he was one, and it was utterly irrational to expect him to act like one, though less irrational to wish he'd put on some more clothes!

Clearly he was of the mindset that said, 'If you've got it, flaunt it.' Her eyes slid down the hard muscled contours of his gleaming torso before she dragged her gaze clear, deeply ashamed of her shallow and ill-timed fascination with his body.

In her defence—he *definitely* had it!

CHAPTER FIVE

'How?'

Neve blinked at him in a dazed fashion and shook her head.

'How are you going to find your sister, Neve Gray Macleod?' he elaborated, voicing the question he had been asking himself since they had reached safety.

Severo had reached the conclusion that his best hope of discovering the youngster was to retrace his steps to the point where he had found her sister. The first step would be persuading this girl that it was a trip he had to make solo.

He could appeal to her reason and explain she would slow him down, or if reason failed—a distinct possibility based on her attitude to this point—he would have to adopt less subtle methods.

He knew his chances of finding the kid were not good, but *not good* was a great deal better than the zero they would be if he did not try.

Only half listening, Neve turned to him. 'What do you mean?'

'It is not a trick question. I mean how are you going to find her?'

He watched as her smooth brow knitted in furrows of consternation and felt his irritation fade away to be replaced by a sudden and uncharacteristic desire to pull her into his arms and tell her it would be all right.

He would make it all right.

Her strong jaw tightened a notch. It was not a promise he could make and even if it had been it was not his place to play her emotional anchor.

'I just will.' Even to her own ears this sounded lame. 'She can't be far away,' Neve reasoned, directing a resentful look up at his lean face.

'Far away from where exactly? Do you have any idea where we are?' The image that flashed through his mind of her still, cold, lifeless body, the soft pink lips blue, made Severo's voice harsher than he had intended as he added grimly, 'Maybe you should consider how much use you're going to be to this Hannah in a body bag, Neve.'

The stark observation drew a gasp from Neve.

He watched her flinch and brushed away the irrational surge of guilt.

If any situation called for brutal, this was it.

'You have to face facts and the fact is you can't do anything but wait and hope—the chances are that unlike you Hannah had the sense to stay in the car and wait to be rescued. The men in the pub said that the last time this happened there were zero casualties.'

Severo preferred to think of it as an invention rather than a lie, and when he saw the flicker of wary hope in her eyes he did not regret abandoning his policy that the truth was always best.

'Really?' Neve *wanted* to believe him. 'You really think it's possible someone found her?'

Her startled eyes opened wide when his big hand moved to frame her face, but she did not pull away. 'I do.'

He projected such total assurance that Neve felt some of the muscle-burning tension between her shoulder blades reduce a notch. For the first time she allowed herself to believe in a 'less than complete disaster' scenario.

'I think it more than likely that your Hannah is even now

sitting somewhere safe and warm worried out of her mind about you.'

Neve was too emotionally drained to think about censoring her response as she gave a shaky laugh and said with total conviction, 'Oh, she won't be.'

She gave a tired sigh and wondered if she would ever be able to convince the troubled and grieving teenager that she was not the enemy.

Severo watched the expressions drift across her extremely expressive face; you could almost hear the thoughts inside her head.

Her transparency fascinated and at the same time appalled him. How, he wondered, could a person go through life with their emotions this close to the surface?

'You and your sister had a falling out?'

'Hannah's not my sister.'

Explaining this reminded her of the occasions when James had been forced to explain that Neve was not his daughter, but his wife. If the marriage had been real and not simply a legal convenience Neve would not have been embarrassed by the raised eyebrows and knowing glances this information frequently produced.

The admission caused the indentation above his hawkish nose to deepen as his hand fell from her face. '*Not* your sister?'

He did not normally make assumptions, but younger sister had seemed to explain the level of her almost hysterical anxiety.

'Hannah is my stepdaughter.' Neve winced inwardly as she registered the defensive note in her voice.

His lean body tensed as an expression she could not decipher flashed across his face.

He wasn't the first to look dubious about the title, but on the plus side she had always found incredulity to be infinitely preferable to the occasional flash of recognition she saw in people's eyes when she explained her relationship to Hannah.

It hadn't actually happened that often, not even at the height of the scandal, probably because the only photo the press had ever managed to take of her had been taken at the funeral.

Wearing a classic black shift dress and equally timeless pearls, her hair slicked smoothly back for the occasion in an elegant chignon, Neve had barely recognised herself.

A mere week later with her hair tucked into a beret, wearing a fifties polka-dot dirndl skirt, flats and a yellow angora cardigan, she had walked unrecognised straight through a crowd of photographers looking for a glimpse of the elegant 'scarlet widow', as they had dubbed her.

Not that it mattered if this stranger placed her, she had more important things to worry about than stressing over the possibility this man thought she was a mercenary gold-digger.

She had taught herself not to care what people thought about her, or at least to tell herself she didn't. It had been the only way to survive the experience. Luckily the public appetite for the scandal had proved short-lived.

Severo's eyes slid to her hand. There was no ring—he would have noticed it when he had noticed her slender fingers and neatly trimmed polish-free nails.

He noticed them again now and found himself thinking about them on his skin. He struggled for the focus, the mental control that normally was no effort for him.

It continued to elude him.

'You're married?' At one level Severo was aware that his level of shock was totally out of proportion with the discovery.

Her lashes lowered in a protective sweep as she nodded and said abruptly, 'I was. He, Hannah's father, is dead.'

Even now she was unable to refer to James as 'my husband'.

Legally he had been but not in any way that really mattered; a good kind friend whom she really missed, yes, but husband? No.

Severo's dark eyebrows shot upwards as a thoughtful expression crossed his face.

'You are a widow?'

Catching himself in the act of stating the obvious yet again, a habit he despised in others, he stopped and changed the subject—or tried to.

'How long?' he asked, telling himself that his fascination stemmed from the fact she looked far too young to be married let alone widowed.

'James died six months ago.'

'And you are left bringing up *his* teenage child.'

She had been anticipating a slightly embarrassed murmur of sympathy as she inevitably received at moments like this; the implied criticism of James she received in its place made her spring angrily to his defence.

'*My* stepdaughter, and for your information it's very rewarding being—'

'A guiding influence?'

Neve bit her lip, flushing at the sardonic interruption. 'All right, I know I make mistakes.'

'Of course you make mistakes.' His eyes slid over the soft contours of her heart-shaped face and he felt his indignation rise. She should be out there enjoying herself—possibly in his bed? 'You're a child yourself,' he said, trying hard not to think about the unchildlike aspects of the body beneath the blanket.

'I'm twenty-four,' she retorted with dignity.

'So old,' he mocked. 'Surely there was someone more suitable?'

Under the circumstances she was in no position to take offence. 'Someone who doesn't let a teenager wander off into a snowstorm, you mean.' She shook her head and pushed away the guilt; it was an indulgence she had no time for right now.

'I thought she drove off at speed.'

She flashed him a smile of deep insincerity and drawled, 'Thanks for reminding me of that. It's at least two minutes since I ran the mental picture where she was crashing into a tree or off a cliff.'

Severo clicked his tongue in irritation. 'You make everything a drama.'

She flung her arms wide in an expansive gesture and loosed a bitter laugh, conscious that hysteria was only another callous comment away. 'And you don't think all this constitutes a drama? You must lead a much more exciting life than I do.'

'Your problem is you have an overactive imagination.' he contended.

Overactive! Was he serious? If she'd allowed her imagination full rein she'd be a basket case by now, and then, she thought grimly, he'd have room to complain.

'It might not be so active if you put a damned shirt on!'

For a split second their glances connected long enough for her to see the flash of heat, the spark of something sensual, before she closed her eyes and thought, Let the floor open up and swallow me.

It didn't and she was left with little choice after a few mortifying moments to open her eyes.

'It's off-putting,' she said, struggling to regain a little dignity as she directed the comment at a point over his left shoulder; she couldn't stop him laughing at her but she didn't have to watch.

What if he wasn't laughing? What if she hadn't imagined the raw sexual hunger in his eyes? The possibility made her stomach dissolve and her heart bang a little louder against the confines of her ribcage.

'My body offends you?'

The comment drew her gaze reluctantly to his face.

His expression of mild surprise did not fool her for a moment; he could hardly be unaware of the effect he had on women clothed or unclothed, and he was palpably enjoying her discomfiture.

'Not *offends* me,' she rebutted. 'I'm not a prude or anything.'

Aware the denial had made her sound more like a prude than anything else she could have said, she bit her lip and added with a flash of angry belligerence, 'Though I'd prefer to be a prude than an exhibitionist.' She allowed her eyes to move in a condemnatory sweep from his feet to his dark head.

That was the plan, at least. The only problem was her eyes did some unscheduled and pretty obvious slowing on the way, causing a ripple of sensation to move through her body.

Why am I acting like a sex-starved bimbo?

'You think I am an exhibitionist?' he asked, sounding mildly curious and not at all offended.

'I think you're...' She stopped, slowly shaking her head as her spurt of anger lost momentum. Unfortunately the motion did not shake loose the sensual fog that lingered on in her brain, making it hard for her to think as she struggled to keep her hormones under control.

'I have no idea what you are,' she admitted, thinking some people might think it would be fun to find out, but she was definitely not one of them.

'Don't worry, I'm harmless—a pillar of the community.'

Sure you are, she thought, refusing to rise to the bait. 'That's a comfort to know.'

'Your stepdaughter—' He stopped and shook his head. *'Dio!'* he ejaculated, his glance sliding over the soft contours of her youthful face. 'It is hard to credit that you're a mother of any kind.'

'Maybe you shouldn't judge by appearances.' Anger sparkled in Neve's eyes as she lifted her chin and began to move past him.

'Maybe I shouldn't,' he agreed.

Neve turned her head. 'What makes you such an expert on the qualities that make a good stepmother anyway?'

'I'm an expert on the qualities that make a bad one.'

Something in his voice made Neve, in the act of walking away, swing back. 'Everyone is,' she said, unable to totally disguise her bitterness. 'We get a lot of bad press.'

'My expertise is more personal. My father remarried when I was ten.' And you are telling her this why, exactly, Severo?

Now the *something* in his voice made sense. 'And you resented her?'

The perceptive comment caused his expression to blank. There were some things he did not share with anyone; he was not about to start now.

'Thank you for that psychological insight,' he drawled, looking anything but grateful for her soft-voiced sympathy. 'But my childhood is not the subject under discussion.' It never had been, which made his introducing it all the more bizarre.

Neve, oblivious to the warning in his voice, asked earnestly, 'Has it occurred to you that your stepmother was trying to do her best?'

'Oh, Livia was trying to do her best.' And her best had been good enough to drive a wedge between father and son.

'I know nothing about your particular circumstances, of course, but—'

'No, you don't, and that situation is not about to change any time soon.' In contrast to his colourless tone and bored expression, the gleam reflected in his dark eyes was nothing short of combustible. 'I suggest you put your own house in order before you share the benefit of your vast wisdom with the rest of us.'

The chilling hauteur in his cutting put-down drove the colour from Neve's face. 'I don't want to share anything with you.'

It afforded her some comfort that her painfully childish response drew an equally immature retort from him.

'Imagine my devastation.' He swore under his breath and

rubbed his temples with his thumbs to relieve the build-up of pressure there, before returning his attention to the redhead, who for some incomprehensible reason felt she had a licence to offer him advice.

The silence stretched as she stood looking at him with blue eyes that gave him a shock every time he saw them, radiating a mixture of defiance, anger and hurt.

'Where are my clothes?'

Eyes like ice drilled into her as he snapped, 'Do not be ridiculous. Sit back down. *You* are not going anywhere.'

But he was, before he gave into the compulsion to drag her into his arms and either throttle her or drive his tongue between those soft, tempting lips. This woman had pushed him closer to losing control than he had ever been in his adult life.

Neve watched, torn between alarm and apprehension as he strode from the room, grabbing his wet jacket from the coat rack as he passed.

Anxiety made her voice shrill as she yelled after him, 'What are you doing? Where are you...?'

An icy gust of wind blew through the room as the outer door was wrenched open. Without a word he vanished out into the darkness.

Neve reached the door as it slammed shut. The second person in one day to prefer a blizzard to her company... A message there, you think, Neve?

She lifted a hand to her head, the faint ironic smile that curved her lips slipping away as she thought, And what am I meant to do now?

Sit and wait, follow...?

Well, at least she didn't have to put up with his company, the man was a total pain, but as the minutes ticked by she began to worry. What if he was lost? What if he was injured? To go off like that, it was immature, it was reckless—he probably wanted to scare her. Well, she didn't care if he killed himself!

Neve's thoughts continued to go around in dizzying circles, her mood swinging from one violent extreme to another until she couldn't stand it for another second.

She had to do something!

She wrenched open the door, catching her breath and drawing the blanket tight across her shoulders as the cold hit her like a solid wall. She was still catching her breath when a voice snarled, '*Madre di Dio!* What are you doing, woman? Get back inside.'

Neve gave a strangled sob of relief as a dark shadow materialised from the snowy blur and formed a broad-shouldered figure who stamped his way into the room, not the injured victim he had become in her feverish imagining but intact, unharmed and projecting more vitality than a man had any right to.

Her initial relief rapidly morphed into anger so intense that for a moment Neve could not speak at all. She stood there feeling the rage pounding in her temples, watching as he shook his head to dislodge the powdery white residue that clung to the dark strands.

As if he'd just taken a gentle stroll to the corner shop!

The sound her bare foot made on the tiles as she stamped brought his head up.

'How stupid are you?'

Another time the look of astonishment that flashed across his face might have amused her, but Neve was beyond seeing the funny side of anything.

'Of all the brainless, crazy stunts! You could have been killed!' she raged, stamping her foot again as her feelings threatened to overcome her. 'I feel guilty enough about just about everything without having your stupid neck to add to the list.'

'So this is all about you,' he drawled. '*Amazing—*' He

stopped mid scathing rebuttal when without warning she began to cry.

Tears he could have coped with, even remained angry through, but Severo found his defences inadequate against the tearless, great gulping sobs that shook her entire body. As he watched her he could almost feel the layers of protective cynicism meticulously built up over the years peeling away.

His hands clenched at his sides, blood dripping unnoticed from the deep graze on his palm as he fought the compulsion to draw her into his arms.

'Don't cry. I'm sorry if I scared you.'

Neve sniffed in response to the abrupt apology and lifted her head. 'I wasn't scared,' she lied, deeply embarrassed by her uncontrolled emotional outburst. 'I was mad, angry. Storming off like that—you could have said what you were doing instead of just running out and—' She paused, a frown forming on her smooth brow. 'What *were* you doing?'

'When setting out on a search and rescue mission, it always helps when you know where you are. I took your advice and went to look for high ground.'

The high ground he had found was a tin-roofed storage shed that had seen better days. His weight added to the several inches of snow it already supported, had caused the roof to cave in.

A dramatic moment!

A slow smile moved across Neve's face as she raised the hem of the bunched blanket and ran to his side. 'You're going to help me find Hannah!'

Looking down into the blue eyes glowing with gratitude raised to him, Severo felt a dangerous rise of emotion tighten in his chest.

He shook his head. 'We have instructions to stay put.'

Her smile slipped. 'What do you mean?'

'I managed to get a signal. I informed the emergency services of the situation.'

Relief rolled over Neve like a wave. 'That's fantastic. You told them about Hannah?'

Severo nodded. 'Their search parties will be looking for her, though as they said there is a possibility that she has already been found or reached safety on her own.'

'They really think so?'

'Their teams have been finding stranded motorists all day. They were not keen on the idea of me mounting my own rescue mission.' And Severo could see the logic of their thinking.

'But surely,' Neve protested, 'their resources are stretched. The more people out helping—'

'Their attitude is people helping will end up being people who need rescuing, and as you rightly pointed out their resources are already stretched...?'

Her face scrunched into an expression of seething frustration. 'But we can't just sit here and do nothing. Let me speak to them.'

'Sorry, not possible, the signal's gone.' Short of rebuilding the destroyed shed, it would stay gone.

Neve's suspicious frown deepened as she watched him begin to unzip his jacket.

'Well, I want to try.'

Severo regarded her with thinly veiled exasperation. 'There's no point—I have told you.'

'How do I even know you contacted them at all? For all I know you might be making it all up.'

The zip parted and his dark head lifted; Severo levelled an incredulous glare at her. '*Making it up?* Would that,' he asked grimly, 'be make it up as in *lying*?'

Neve pressed a hand to her throat, refusing to give an inch in the face of his icy-eyed anger. 'It's obvious you didn't want to help me find Hannah,' she claimed, in a breathy accusing rush.

Severo made no attempt to defend himself from the angry

charge as he continued to cautiously ease off the jacket that had been all that was protecting his naked torso from the elements and the jagged pieces of torn metal that had cushioned his fall.

Neve, who interpreted his unfriendly silence as a tacit admission of guilt, regarded him with unconcealed contempt that morphed into horror when he finally managed to remove his jacket and revealed the damage it had hidden.

'You're hurt!'

He glanced down in response to her exclamation, his manner dismissive as his eyes brushed across the grazed area on his muscle-ridged belly and the angry raised red welts that ran along the golden skin of his right shoulder. He flexed his shoulder and realised the damage extended to his back.

He'd been, Severo decided, lucky.

'It is superficial.' Though admittedly the deep cut on his palm might need a couple of stitches, or failing that a dressing to stem the blood that still seeped from the jagged edges.

'Superficial!' And he called her stoic! 'Here, sit down. Let me—'

He ignored the chair she had dragged out for him to sit in with an irritable, 'I do not need a ministering angel.'

Neve, jogging to keep pace with his long-legged stride, followed him into the living room, noticing as she did the trail of blood on the floor.

'You're bleeding!' she cried in alarm. The violent strength of her emotions that rose up inside her as she saw the blood dripping from his arm froze Neve to the spot.

He flung her an impatient scowl over his shoulder. 'It's only my hand.'

Like that made it all right, she thought, watching as he grabbed a clean tea towel and wrapped the chequered fabric tightly around the injured area.

Her own hand trembled as she pushed a skein of fiery hair back from her brow. 'And let me guess—it doesn't hurt at all?'

She narrowed her eyes and thought, God save me from stupid macho men!

The macho man in question maintained a stubborn silence as he added another tea towel to the makeshift dressing. Blood was already oozing through the first one; Neve had to look away from the red stain.

Looking at the raised welts that stood out livid on the smooth skin of his brown back made her feel just as bad. She pressed a hand to her stomach where her muscles quivered in sympathetic reaction to his pain.

'What happened? How did you do this?'

'I was on a roof when it collapsed.'

The casual explanation sent a chill through Neve. 'You could have been killed!'

'As you see, I wasn't.' The fact that she was becoming visibly agitated over something that had *not* happened baffled him.

His offhand manner made Neve, who was struggling to banish the image of his broken, lifeless body from her head, see red. 'What on earth,' she yelled, 'were you doing on a *roof*?'

Wasn't a blizzard challenge enough for this man? Did he have to go out looking for alternative ways to kill himself?

'There must be a first-aid kit here somewhere…' she muttered, opening a cupboard door and scanning the neatly arranged contents.

'I was finding the *high ground* and making the phone call that I invented.'

The explanation stopped Neve in her tracks. 'Oh!' She swallowed and gave a shamefaced grimace as she closed the door and straightened up empty-handed.

Feeling several kinds of a fool, she glanced warily up at his lean face. 'I suppose I owe you an apology.'

'I suppose so too.'

If she had hoped to see some thawing in his manner, Neve

was disappointed. 'I'm sorry about what I said...I suppose I was a bit...'

He angled a sardonic brow and watched the colour in her cheeks deepen.

'Paranoid?' she suggested.

'Yes, you were.' He left his task long enough to sling her a curious look from under the sweep of his ridiculously long lashes. 'Are you always this freakishly obsessive when you get an idea in your head?'

Under the circumstances she could hardly take offence at the question, and she had in her life been accused of tunnel vision. 'Hannah's my responsibility.'

'You asked your stepdaughter to steal a car and run away?'

'No, of course not.'

He arched an eloquent brow.

'But I'm the adult.'

'I doubt if that would make a difference.' His assessing glance moved across her face. 'I can see you at two, beating yourself up when your teddy bear lost an ear and feeling responsible when your best friend fell over and cut her knee.'

'Don't be ridiculous.' She stopped, an arrested expression spreading slowly across her face as she realised there was more than a grain of truth in his comments.

Hadn't she always been the responsible one, first trying to keep Charlie out of trouble, and herself out of the care system? And now there was Hannah.

'You have to take responsibility for your own actions,' she asserted stubbornly.

Neve had been doing that since she was fourteen.

The year her parents had been killed in the train crash.

Officially Charlie had been her guardian after their parents' deaths, but Charlie's ideas of guardianship had not been strictly conventional.

Charlie would vanish for weeks at a time, often after saying he was just popping to the shop for a loaf of bread. It had made her self-reliant and also a pretty good liar!

She'd had no choice. If the authorities had suspected she was living alone for weeks and sometimes months at a stretch they would have swooped, and being taken into care was one of Neve's nightmares.

It was her own teenage years that had made her empathise with Hannah's situation—not, of course, that Hannah would ever find herself in a position where she had to live on sardines on toast for a week and say she didn't want to go to the cinema with her friends because she didn't have any money.

'The responsibility is no longer yours, *cara*. The professionals are on the job. Take a back seat and let it go.' It was easy to see that letting go was an alien concept to her.

Neve bit her lip. 'But—'

He held up his uninjured hand. 'You're not in control. Why not enjoy the experience?'

The astonishing suggestion drew her incredulous gaze to his face. 'Enjoy!' she echoed, repeating the concept to herself. Enjoy being stranded God knew where with a beautiful, devastatingly handsome stranger—actually when you put it like that she realised there were more than a few women who would pay for the experience!

'A smile,' he approved. 'That's an improvement. Think of it as an adventure. How many people get the opportunity to escape the real world even for a few hours? No stress, no responsibilities, no emails or phone.' He had convinced himself but the redhead's expression suggested she would be a harder nut to crack.

Neve compressed her lips into a prim line. 'I don't like adventures.'

'There are many kinds of adventures, *cara*.'

The low, intimate drawl sent a shivery shudder through her body. She had no intention of even trying to translate the meaning lurking in that seemingly innocent observation.

Instead she dragged her gaze free of his bold, uncomfortably perceptive stare and abruptly changed the subject, asking in a bright voice, 'Can I do something to help? The wounds should be cleaned.' Even before the words had left her lips she was panicking about the thought of touching him, and not just because the idea of hurting him made her stomach churn.

'Thanks for the offer, but I think the easiest way to clean these—' he flexed his shoulder experimentally and struggled to repress a wince '—is to take a shower.'

'Good idea!' she enthused, relieved that her offer had been rejected.

'I hope there's hot water.' Though possibly under the circumstances cold might be more appropriate. His icy adventure had not lessened the lust that had him firmly in its grip.

The night ahead held a lot of interesting possibilities. He felt some of his tiredness fall away as he climbed the stairs and considered them.

CHAPTER SIX

UNABLE to stop following him with her eyes, Neve watched until Severo vanished from view.

She still hadn't moved when a few moments later she heard the sound of water running, loudly, as though he hadn't bothered to close the door behind him.

Some people might take that as an invitation to join him.

Neve gave a shocked groan and closed her eyes, her face scrunched into a grimace as she folded her arms onto the counter top. With a sigh she rested her head on them and struggled to eject the sybaritic image of the tall Italian standing under the spray, the warm jets of water cascading over his brown skin.

What is wrong with me?

Up until this point, focused on Hannah, she had been able to block out the effect that Severo Constanza had on her. Now she was forced to reluctantly confront the situation.

She was attracted to him, and why not? He looked incredible—definitely the sexiest man she had ever encountered. She would have to be dead from the neck down not to be affected by his brand of raw sexuality!

It wasn't as though it was anything deep and meaningful, and it wasn't as though she would ever do anything about it.

She found him sexually attractive, but she found lightning storms attractive too—she didn't have to go outside to feel the crackle of electricity in the air and risk getting struck to enjoy their raw primal beauty. She could do that from the safety of a warm room.

Severo was good to look at, but touching was definitely off the agenda.

Even if the opportunity arose?

His comments about escaping the real world surfaced in her head. Following this logic, did that mean that the normal rules were suspended? Could a person think or even do things in this little bubble that they wouldn't normally consider?

Neve shut off this internal dialogue with a shocked gasp. What she needed was something to keep her busy, keep those dangerous thoughts at bay.

Frowning, she looked around the room thinking, But what?

This was a cook's kitchen, she decided, studying the rows of spice bottles and shelves of cook books. Neve always found baking therapeutic in moments of stress and eating could be comforting. This was definitely a moment of stress and, while a batch of cookies was the first thing to come to mind, it wasn't the most nourishing.

She adjusted the blanket, wrapping it sarong-style to free up her hands before she walked to the fridge and pulled open the door. After examining the contents of the well-stocked shelves she removed a box of eggs and the ingredients to produce a veggie omelette.

Easing her conscience, she made a list of the items she had removed, then, promising herself she would replace them at a later date, she began to slice and dice before whipping the eggs with more vigour than was strictly required.

The thing would only take a few minutes to throw together and cook when he returned.

Stifling a yawn, she moved across to the chair by the fire she had vacated earlier. Within seconds she felt her mind drift.

* * *

He wanted her.

Severo could not recall ever having wanted a woman more—and he would definitely have remembered! She was beautiful, but not the type of woman he was usually attracted to, yet— Severo stopped, conscious that he was beginning to sound like one of those men he had always despised, the ones who analysed their feelings and motivations.

The important thing was he was not and never would be a man like his father. Severo did not lose control and make a fool of himself over a pretty face. He did not confuse sex with love; he frequently doubted the latter existed outside the pages of fiction.

The strength of the desire burning in his blood was clearly a result of his prolonged period of celibacy.

It had been over six months since he had walked away from his last relationship, too long for any man to go without sex.

The relationship had not ended well. The final showdown had been messy and shrill, involving a lot of frankly bizarre accusations from April. It had been distasteful and not an experience he had been anxious to repeat in a hurry.

The problem was women said one thing when they meant another. April was a classic case: she had announced herself more than happy when he had explained that he was not look-ing for anything permanent or intense.

Uncomplicated, no-strings sex, she had told him, was all she wanted from a relationship.

Only it turned out she had wanted other things too.

Things like expecting him to attend boring social events and be nice to people he did not know or like. He had been willing to humour her to a degree because she was very beau-tiful and skilled in the bedroom and he could see that her career depended on her being seen at the right places. But when it came to her wanting to know where he was every second of the day he had not been so obliging.

The final straw had been when she had started talking marriage and babies; jokingly, of course, but she hadn't been.

Nobody was that good in bed!

An image of the sexy pouting curve of Neve's full lips flashed into his head as he entered the room—he was willing to be proved wrong.

But not just yet, it seemed.

His expression set in a discontented scowl of frustration, he walked over to where she lay curled up like a kitten, her face cushioned on her arm, dead to the world.

Expression taut, he dragged his uninjured hand through his damp hair and took the opportunity to study her sleeping face at his leisure.

His scowl faded.

The soft tumble of bright silky coils of hair spilled over her slender shoulders, her sleeping face was flushed, her lashes cast a shadow on the peachy curve of her smooth flushed cheek. His lust surged back full force as his glance stilled on her mouth.

She was beautiful and Severo had never experienced a more primal need to claim a woman for his own.

Neve had no recollection of falling asleep, just the smell of coffee, then opening her eyes and finding herself in a strange candle-lit room.

She sensed his disturbing presence before she heard his voice. 'So you are back with us.'

Tall and lean and wearing a towelling robe that ended mid muscular calf, he loomed over her.

'Why did you let me sleep?' she demanded accusingly.

He nearly hadn't—the temptation to kiss her awake had been strong, but he had managed to resist.

'You obviously needed it.' Not as much as he needed to sink his tongue between her parted lips. 'Are you always this cranky when you wake up?' It would, he decided, be interesting to find out.

Frowning as she eased a few kinks out of her spine, Neve ignored the question and levelled a glare at his cleanly shaven face. 'Why the candles?'

'A fuse blew while you were asleep, but luckily only the one responsible for the lights. We still have power and heating, so we won't have to resort to sharing body heat to keep warm.'

His mockery caused embarrassed colour to fly to her face. The other reactions of her body to the image that flashed into her head were happily less obvious, but equally humiliating.

'Can't you fix a fuse?' she asked, injecting scorn into her voice.

'Possibly, if I could find the fuse box.'

Neve was extremely suspicious of this uncharacteristic show of helplessness.

'Did you even try?' she accused, lifting a hand to her head as she watched him pad barefoot across to the fire.

While he wasn't watching she took the opportunity to smooth her tousled hair. As she rubbed a strand of hair from her cheek she felt the creases. Great—not only had her hair gone feral, there was the imprint of the chair arm on her face.

He threw a log on the fire before replying to her question. 'No, I like the romantic ambience, and candlelight is so forgiving,' he mocked.

She let her hand fall from her face. Ironically he had a point: being in the presence of perfection made a person awfully aware of her own deficiencies. It seemed most unfair that while he was wandering around looking sexy and gorgeous she was sitting there looking like a madwoman with her creased face and her wild hair—not to mention wearing a blanket.

'You warm enough?' he asked, studying her flushed cheeks and feverishly bright eyes.

Conscious of the prickle of nervous sweat trickling down her spine, Neve nodded and lied. 'I'm fine.'

She would be a lot finer if she were wearing more than her bra and pants. Her state of undress made her feel vulnerable and exposed; the idea of putting on the wet clothes she had removed was not pleasant but it beat the alternative.

'Where are my clothes?' She glanced around, trying to conceal her growing agitation behind a cool façade and, she suspected, failing miserably. 'What have you done with them?'

His ebony brows lifted in response to the shrill note of accusation that crept into her voice.

'Not really my size, *cara*, but I admire your bold take on colour co-ordination.'

Neve's glance slid to the impressive width of his shoulders as she sketched a mirthless smile. 'Very amusing.'

'Relax, I put them in the drier with my things.'

'Very domesticated.'

'I have my moments.'

Neve swallowed and thought, I bet you do. The images in her head of him enjoying *moments* with a whole succession of nubile leggy blondes made her feel queasy.

'Oh, except for this,' he said, unfolding the thin strappy top from the rail of the range cooker where he'd draped it.

Neve watched in dismay, unable to control the visible shudder that ran through her body as he rubbed the silky fabric between his long fingers.

'Warm and dry,' he said before he tossed it to her.

Neve dropped her gaze from the glittering challenge in his as she reached out and grabbed for it, losing her purchase on the blanket as she did so. Her top in her fist, she pulled up the blanket from her waist, where it had slipped.

The glimpse of her pale body sent a surge of lust through Severo's already painfully aroused body. It was so extreme that for a moment the man who was famed for his hard-nosed cool temperament could not breathe.

Cloaked by the blanket, she fought her way into her top. Conscious of his dark eyes trained on her, she grumbled, 'I suppose it would be too much to expect you to turn your back?'

'Most women with your body would be glad of the opportunity to flaunt it.'

His sarcasm *shouldn't* have hurt because, while she didn't have any hang-ups about her body, Neve had no illusions either.

'I need my clothes.'

He smiled and slowly shook his head. 'No, *cara*, you need—'

'I don't need anything you can offer!'

He looked mildly surprised by the spitting rancour of her interruption. 'I was about to say food. I thought you might be hungry.'

Neve swallowed as the mortified colour rushed to her face. 'Oh!'

'I enjoyed my omelette.' His glance swept the dishes waiting to go into the dishwasher. 'I thought you might like one too. After that we can play it by ear.'

Ignoring the worrying postscript but unwilling to call him on it and make an utter fool of herself for a second time, she focused her tight-lipped response on the food portion of his plan.

'I'm not hungry, and you shouldn't be cooking with that hand. It'll start bleeding if you knock it.' As there appeared to be nothing covering it she was surprised it hadn't done so already.

'No, it won't,' he contradicted, looking smug as he extended his injured hand towards her.

Neve's eyes shot wide as she took in the neat row of stitches across his palm. The extreme form of DIY made her jaw drop. Her amazed eyes flew to his face.

'You actually sewed up your own hand?'

'The damned thing wouldn't stop bleeding so when I spotted a sewing kit in the bathroom—being ambidextrous is on occasion useful.'

'Do you do this often, then?'

He flashed her a grin, looking amused by her comment. 'I actually think I didn't do such a bad job,' he remarked, turning his hand to admire his own handiwork. He angled her a questioning look. 'What do you think?'

She stared at his long, tapering fingers; he had beautiful hands. 'Think?' she croaked, seeing his long, sensitive fingers sliding over her skin. 'I think you're slightly mad.' *And I am totally and completely insane.*

Maybe I have a fever?

Oh, you have a fever, all right, but not the sort that an aspirin is going to cure.

His eyes drifted to her mouth and he felt the ache in his groin intensify. He smiled into her blue eyes and felt a surge of predatory satisfaction as her pupils dilated dramatically, almost swallowing up the blue.

'You might be right, *cara*.'

The primitive, sexually explicit message glowing in his dark eyes sent a surge of lustful longing through her body.

Gripped by panic, she redirected her attention to his hand and pretended to study his handiwork. 'It is neat,' she agreed. 'Very professional. Maybe,' she suggested lightly, 'you missed your true calling. Why didn't you become a doctor?'

The reference drew his brows into a straight frowning line above his hawkish nose. 'How did you know?'

'You said you did pre-med.'

'So I did—good memory,' he murmured admiringly. 'I quit

school when my father died. I inherited the family firm, so to speak.' And discovered a talent for making money, which was fortunate as the coffers had been pretty low at the time.

'Do you regret it?'

'It was expected, and I don't do regrets.'

Neve was not convinced. 'Everyone does regrets.'

He produced an enigmatic smile. 'What about you?'

'Me?'

'What do you do, Neve? I'm curious—are you a career criminal or was it an opportunist crime?'

Neve gave a perplexed shake of her head. 'I don't understand?'

'It was my car you stole. You walked straight into me in the pub car park.'

A memory stirred; she recalled the tall figure in the car park. 'You were in my way.'

His lips quirked; that was certainly one way to look at it.

'And you stole my car.'

He leaned back against the wall and watched as a tide of warmth worked its way under her clear pale skin leaving it tinged with a pink rosiness.

'It was an emergency and I only meant to borrow it.'

'I am not sure borrowing a stranger's car is recognized, legally speaking, though I believe that the courts are generally fairly lenient with first-time offenders. Are you?' he taunted.

'This isn't funny. It's not a joke.' Especially not if the police did become involved. 'I'm very sorry about your car.' Did this mean that her rescue had not been accidental?

Again he seemed to read her thoughts.

'There were some valuable items in the car I wanted to retrieve.'

'Sorry,' she whispered, feeling guiltier than ever. 'I didn't think.' The excuse sounded pretty lame even to her own ears. 'I just panicked. I ran outside and my car was gone. I realised that Hannah must have taken it and your car was there and unlocked…which was pretty stupid if you had valuables in it.'

'So it was actually my fault.'

The shamed colour flew to her cheeks. 'No, of course not, it's *my* fault.'

'Your stepdaughter will never learn to take responsibility for her own actions if you constantly blame yourself.'

Neve's blue eyes flew wide. *'Hannah!'* Shame washed over her like a dark tide. Until he had mentioned her she had momentarily forgotten her stepdaughter's plight.

His dark eyes softened as he studied her face. 'I assume you had a falling out?'

That, she thought, was like calling a nuclear explosion a loud bang.

A self-condemnatory frown formed on her smooth brow as she gnawed worriedly at her lower lip and admitted, 'She was running away from me.'

Her tortured gaze was drawn to the window as she gulped and, embarrassed, turned away to hide the tears that sprang to her eyes.

Severo was conscious of some unidentifiable emotion swelling in his chest as he watched her reach out a finger and trace a pattern in the mist on the window.

He shook his head and told himself not to look for complications where there were none. This was not about spiritual connections; it was about scheduling and sex.

Work had been frantic for the last few months but this was clearly his body's way of telling him he needed to make some time in his schedule to redress the balance.

All work and no play made Jack, or in this instance Severo, a man apt to become unhealthily fixated by blue eyes… As for fantasising about a woman's skin or wanting to drive the sadness from her face, that was simply just not him!

'I'm sure your Hannah is fine.'

They both remained motionless as their eyes met in the reflected image on the window.

The moment stretched, the heavy silence seething with unspoken words. Neve felt light-headed; awareness hummed in her blood and prickled hotly under her skin. She could feel the heavy throb of tension as it built and took on a presence that felt physical.

A log in the fire exploded with a soft hiss, breaking the spell. She gave a small gasp and, flushing, turned around to face him.

'Not knowing,' she said bleakly. 'It's awful. I...'

She stopped as his hand came down heavily on her shoulders.

'Don't think of it.'

CHAPTER SEVEN

THAT was the problem: she hadn't been.

The guilty knowledge of her selfishness ate away at Neve like acid. Until Severo had said her name she had not thought about Hannah.

She'd dreamt about him when she slept and from the moment she had woken her thoughts had revolved exclusively around this man.

Tucking the errant strands of hair behind her ears, she pulled away and eyed him with burning blue-eyed resentment.

'You make it sound easy.' It wasn't meant to be this easy. I am just shallow and self-obsessed.

'I don't think it is easy, just necessary.'

Neve compressed her lips. He didn't have a clue about the burden of responsibility she felt or the guilt or…the man was a damned computer! 'I need my clothes.'

Severo swore under his breath, frustration stamped on his autocratic features as he watched her stalk stiff-backed from the room.

Neve squinted as her eyes adjusted to the darkness in the laundry room, but after carefully feeling her way along the counter top she located what she was looking for. Kneeling on the tiled floor, wincing a little because it was very cold, she opened the door of the drier and caught the garments that spilled out in her arms. They were dry but tangled.

She nodded encouragement to herself as she succeeded in

detaching her jeans from a shirt—not hers. One second she was incuriously scanning the discreet hand-sewn designer label, the next she was responding to some inexplicable but strong impulse and pressing the fine cotton to her face. Her eyes closed as she inhaled the clean male scent that seemed impregnated into the creased fabric.

What am I doing?

Eyes wide in recognition of her truly bizarre behaviour, she stopped and dropped the offending garment. The other thing she had been doing was holding her breath; she released it now in a long shuddering sigh and, spotting some pink polka-dot fabric, reached for her sweater. The male sock it had wrapped itself around came with it.

On the plus side, she was not going to be tempted to sniff a sock.

'Has it shrunk?'

Even had he possessed a working knowledge of care labels, Severo had had other things on his mind when he had piled the sodden garments into the machine earlier.

At the sound of his deep voice Neve released a startled gasp of shock and spun around, her bottom making contact with the floor with a thud as she lost her balance and tipped over backwards.

He grimaced, but all Neve could see from where she sat was a flash of white teeth bared, in her mind at least, in a heartless wolfish smirk.

'That must have hurt.'

It had, and it was also very cold, but Neve was not about to admit it to the figure who was sitting on one of the bottom treads of the polished staircase in the adjoining room, his position offering him an excellent view of her furtive actions.

She held onto her sweater like a lifeline as she clutched it to her heaving chest and glared at him.

Her glittering electric-blue eyes reminded him of a Siamese

cat an ex girlfriend had carried around in a designer bag, until the animal had scratched her.

Neve's nails were neat and short and she wore no jewellery.

His ex had kept the jewelled collar she had made the poor animal wear, but got rid of the animal after the incident. It had scratched him too, displaying feline ingratitude when, saving it from the fate his girlfriend had in mind, Severo had gifted it to the cat-loving daughter of his secretary.

Neve found the contemplative smile that tugged at the corners of his sensual mouth unsettling. 'What are you smiling at?' she demanded spikily.

The image of a jewelled collar, sapphires to match her eyes set against her fair skin in his head, Severo produced one of his inimitable shrugs. 'I'm a naturally smiley sort of guy.'

Neve snorted at this patent untruth and continued to view him with wary suspicion.

Just how long had he been there watching her anyhow?

She wasn't aware she had voiced the question out loud until he leaned forward and, resting his elbows on his knees, propped his chin on one hand and drawled, 'Long enough.'

Neve did not want to know if 'long enough' meant he had seen her breathing in the fragrance of his clothes like some demented bloodhound.

'I got lonely.' The mockery he had intended to inject into the statement failed to materialise as he was gripped by an urgent and compelling desire to hold, to touch, to taste.

A need that seemed to override every atom of common sense he possessed.

Neve, who was utterly oblivious to the strained edge in his cryptic response, lifted her chin, frowning as she struggled to stay focused and not allow herself to be fatally distracted by the aura of masculinity he projected.

She failed miserably. Just looking at him filled her with an inarticulate longing so intense that her bones ached with it.

Severo swallowed and, breathing through flared nostrils, exhaled slowly before asking quietly, 'Are you going to tell me what is wrong now?'

She shrugged and, frustrated, he swore audibly in his native tongue as he moved to join her. 'I don't enjoy scenes, Neve.'

'And you think I do?' Over the past few months she had had a gut full of scenes; Hannah took delight in humiliating her, frequently venting her anger in public.

She was struggling to her feet when big hands closed around her waist and hauled her upright.

For the space of several seconds she was suspended two feet off the ground as if she weighed no more than a rag doll. While she was dangling in mid-air her eyes locked with his dark compelling stare.

She did not have time to either enjoy or reject the rush in her blood or the prickle under her skin before she was placed on her own feet. Earthbound at least physically, her head was still spinning, but then she had never had a head for heights or, as it turned out, tall, impossibly sexy Italians with dark fallen-angel faces. The faint buzzing in her head got louder as her glance slid to the sternly sensual outline of his mouth.

A dreamy expression filtered into her sapphire eyes as a dragging sensation low in her pelvis made her breath quicken. The thought popped fully formed into her head before she could stop it—with a mouth like that he had to be an excellent kisser.

Deeply ashamed that she could think such a thought when Hannah was out there hurt, or worse, she lowered her lashes in a protective sweep, feeling the heat climb up her neck until her cheeks burned with shame.

He gave a sigh and, studying her down-bent head, felt a sudden strong inclination to thread his fingers into that fiery mass and pull back her head to expose the lovely line of her smooth white throat.

She presented him her rigid back before bending to pick up the clothes from the drier.

Peachy was the most applicable word, he decided, studying the outline of her firm little bottom against the softly draped cloth. The knowledge she wore very little underneath drove him crazy.

She bent forward a little more and the fabric slid higher, revealing more of her slim, creamy smooth thighs. The pounding in his temples stepped up another notch as Severo watched the mental image of his fingers gliding across her soft warm belly, making his eyes darken to midnight black.

Having now reclaimed all her clothes, his lying on the floor in a crumpled heap, Neve turned with them bundled in her arms. She shot a look of anger up at him through her damp lashes.

Their glances connected and Neve, painfully conscious of things tightening and shifting deep inside her, swallowed.

'If it was your child out there you wouldn't say don't think about her.'

He frowned, not understanding her reference. 'I have no child.'

This was not a situation that Severo saw a need to alter any time soon. Call him old-fashioned but to his mind a man needed a wife to have a child, and to commit yourself to someone for the rest of your life was more than a leap in the dark; it was, to his way of thinking, a form of insanity!

He was not saying there were no happy marriages, but marriage was, when you viewed it logically, a lottery. The problem was that the participants rarely viewed it logically when they entered into it with all sorts of unreasonable and irrational expectations.

His dark features swam, blurred by tears, as Neve lifted her gaze to his face. 'I know you were trying to help.'

The anger that had drawn the skin taut across his strong-boned features faded at the husky admission.

'I'm not angry with you, I'm angry...actually,' she corrected with a shudder of distaste, 'I'm *disgusted* with me.'

His brows lifted at her choice of words. 'I doubt very much that you have done anything so very disgusting, *cara*.'

Neve shook her head, too ashamed to look at him as she pleaded, 'Don't be nice to me!' She swallowed and added in a small voice, 'I don't deserve it.'

'I will not be nice to you,' Severo agreed, contemplating her down-bent head with narrowed eyes as he added coolly, 'But I will shake you if you don't stop all this hair-shirt nonsense.'

This brought her head up with a jerk. It was not a threat of retribution she saw in his dark eyes, but something that approached tenderness.

'You're being nice!' she accused.

Severo's jaw tightened as he struggled to contain his growing frustration. 'I could be a lot nicer if you allowed me.'

Too caught up in her orgy of self-recrimination Neve, barely registering his throaty comment, cut across him.

'No, you don't understand. I made that big song and dance about finding Hannah, and then I forgot her.'

'Cut yourself some slack. You're exhausted.'

Neve shook her head. 'I forgot her because I can't stop...' She swallowed and lifted her tragically swimming blue eyes to his. 'I was thinking about you,' she revealed.

After a moment's shock—this was the last thing he had expected to hear her say—Severo felt a surge of savage satisfaction.

Neve shook her head, dropped her head into her hands and let out a self-recriminatory growl of disgust. 'And I don't even like you.'

His dark, thickly lashed eyes glittered. 'Liking is not necessary for what we are feeling, *cara*.'

Neve's head slowly lifted. She sniffed and searched his face warily. What she saw there made her heart skip several beats. *'We?'*

'*Per amor di Dio*, you are not going to tell me that you do not know I badly want to get you into bed?'

The sexual buzz in the air hummed as their glances connected, blue on smouldering sloe black.

'I was…I'm not, I don't do one-night stands.' Just looking at him made her bones ache with desire. 'I shouldn't even be thinking about it, not with Hannah out—'

He touched a silencing finger to her lips. 'Thinking about sex does not mean you have stopped caring, or that you have become some selfish monster.'

Neve envied his confidence on this subject.

'Thinking about sex,' he confided huskily, 'is as natural as having sex.' But not nearly as satisfying.

Neve did not feel qualified to offer an opinion on a subject on which she was totally ignorant.

'But I—'

'I know.'

'You do?' she said, staring up into his face. He really was the most incredible-looking man, she thought, her gaze sliding over the carved planes and angles, fascinated by the length of his eyelashes, the razor-edged perfection of his cheekbones.

A man like this wants me?

'You still feel married, but the fact is you are not. How long ago…six months, did you say?'

Neve, who had never *felt* married, nodded.

She wondered what he would say if she told him she had felt trapped.

Trapped in a loveless marriage of convenience.

'And during that time there have been no men?'

Indignant colour rushed to her face. 'Of course not!' She was about to add 'no men full stop ever' when he spoke.

'I too have had no sex for a similar period.'

'*You!*'

He accepted her amazement with a shrug of his magnificent shoulders. 'It is not usual,' he admitted. 'And celibacy suits me no more than it does you. But there were reasons, which I will not bore you with,' he added, giving just enough information to arouse her curiosity.

'We have appetites, we find ourselves here alone, isolated—it is hardly surprising that we have been drawn to each other.'

'You're drawn to me?'

'I want sex with you.' A nerve clenched beside his jaw as he added starkly, 'Badly.'

Did that mean he wanted bad sex or he wanted sex badly? The sound of his gravelly voice pitched low, almost a whisper, made the downy hairs on her skin stand on end, or was that the stroking movement of his thumb on her cheek?

'This is wrong,' she whispered, struggling with the last dregs of her strength to drag herself clear of the sensual vortex she felt herself being sucked into. 'Hannah is out there somewhere and I can't just—'

'How will this hurt Hannah?'

'It won't, but—'

He pressed a finger to her mouth. 'No buts. You do know you have the most incredible eyes.' His big body was curved over her in an almost possessive manner, so close that she could feel the heat from his lean body, smell the soap he must have used earlier and, overlying that citrusy tang, the male musky scent of his body.

Neve knew her knees were shaking but she felt strangely disconnected from her body; she couldn't tear her gaze free of the hypnotic stare of his heavy lidded eyes.

'Nothing is going to happen if you don't want it to, *cara*.'

She closed her eyes and shook her head. Hannah was her responsibility. James had asked her to look after his daughter and after all the things he had done for her it was not such a big ask. She had promised James she'd look after her and she had failed.

Severo felt her stiffen and swore softly under his breath. 'Stop thinking.'

'I c...can't.'

'Then think about my mouth,' he said, still looking at her eyes.

'*Your mouth?*' she echoed, her wide eyes automatically zeroing in on the sculpted sensual curve. They refused to move on. She just carried on staring. There was a distant buzzing in her head and the sound of someone breathing hard.

Is that me?

'I've thought,' she croaked, still staring. 'And, all right, you have a pretty amazing mouth, though I'm sure you've heard that before.'

'I like your mouth too.'

His deep voice had a tactile quality. A little of the cry locked in her throat escaped as a small mewling sound; she felt the beads of sweat break out across her skin as he bent his head closer.

She wanted to move but none of her muscles responded to the desperate commands being issued a secret part of her didn't want them to.

Her eyes stayed wide and she didn't move an inch as he fitted his mouth to her own.

His lips were cool and firm, the pressure light.

The contact only lasted a moment before he broke it, lifting his face but staying close enough for her to see the gold tips on his eyelashes and the fine lines radiating from the corners of his eyes.

Breathing hard, each breath a conscious effort, Neve just carried on staring at him. Everything seemed to have slowed—the thud of her heart, the hissing sound of her breath—as she struggled to drag air into her lungs.

'Think of my lips.'

His voice, dark and textured like bitter chocolate, seemed to come from a long way off.

His head dipped. 'My tongue,' he rasped, beginning to trace the trembling outline of her full upper lip, leaving a tingling damp trail and his taste.

Neve's hands tightened into fists as a whimper was dragged from somewhere deep inside her.

'Nothing else exists,' he whispered in the same insidiously seductive whisper. 'Just taste and texture, heat and moisture.'

'Oh, God!' she moaned as his teeth tugged gently at the curve of her lower lip. His breath was warm on her face. She struggled to gather her scattered wits. 'I think—'

He pressed a finger to her lips and shook his head. 'No, do not think, just feel, taste and enjoy. Don't worry, you'll get the hang of it—all you need is practice.'

Staring into his dark eyes and feeling dizzy, she swallowed. 'This is silly.' Surreal, silly and probably dangerous; she felt as if she might have a heart attack at any moment. The pounding in her chest was deafening and she could hardly breathe.

She shuddered as he kissed the corner of her mouth, then he moved along the curve nipping and tasting, tracing it with his tongue.

She stood there, her eyes half closed, her lashes brushing against the feverish flush along the crest of her cheekbones, feeling the warm currents of sensation sliding through her body growing until the warmth tipped over into a flash fire that made her heat; she was burning up!

It was dark, delicious torture.

CHAPTER EIGHT

'DON'T stop,' Neve gasped against his mouth and was rewarded with a hard kiss.

Supporting her head with his hand, Severo applied the sweet crushing pressure that made bright lights explode behind Neve's closed eyelids.

She felt him pull away, but she could still hear him breathing hard; it was difficult to separate the sound from the pounding rush of blood in her ears.

She shuddered and forced her heavy eyelids open, fighting the enervating weakness that made every movement an effort.

'Well, that was nice while it lasted, but you can't kiss me all night.' The glitter of his smoky eyes made her head spin; she shivered as he ran a finger down her cheek and slurred her name.

Appearing to like the sound of it, he said it again, rolling it over his tongue, making it sound like a caress. There was a fascinated expression on his face as he smoothed back the bright hair from her brow.

'*Dio mio,*' he rasped, 'you have no idea what I can do, *cara.*'

Neve shivered, believing implicitly the unspoken promise in his arrogant claim.

'Am I going to find out?' she whispered, amazed at her own recklessness. A sense of freedom she had never experienced before surged through Neve's veins. He was right—this wasn't hurting anyone.

'Would you like to?'

'Do you do everything else as well as you kiss?'

He laughed, throwing back his head and revealing the strong brown column of his throat. 'I haven't kissed you yet. I've not even tasted you.' But he was going to and the anticipation of sliding his tongue into that soft sweet heat sent a hard shudder through his body.

She gazed at his dark face with an expression of rapt fascination—how could any man be that utterly gorgeous? How could any man make her bones ache with need?

Maybe it was just this one?

Her heart was thudding so loud that she could hardly hear herself as she whispered, 'What was that if it wasn't a kiss?'

He smiled against her mouth, rubbing the side of his nose against hers as he tugged at her full pink under lip with his teeth. 'Foreplay.'

A gush of molten anticipation slid through Neve's body as his dark head dipped. Her lips parted; the submissive symbolism of the gesture drew a deep feral groan from Severo.

'*Dio*, but you taste so good…'

Neve did not understand the rest of his husky words as he slid seamlessly into his native tongue, but the repetitive stabbing incursion of his tongue as he explored the warm recesses of her mouth needed no translation.

She kissed him back with a blind desperation that was beyond anything she had imagined. Incapable of resisting and not wanting to, she gave into the primal heat coursing through her blood and met his tongue with her own.

Then, when it wasn't enough, with a driven moan she grabbed his head, sliding her fingers into the thick lush pelt of his hair.

He responded, kissing her with bruising pressure that

arched her spine backwards. The heat flared white-hot between them as they kissed, not gently, but with a mutual desperation that left no room for conscious thought.

When they finally broke apart they were both gasping for air.

If he let her go Neve was sure she would slide to the floor. 'Don't let me go. I don't think I can stand up.'

He gave a smile that made her heart flip, trailed a kiss with slow, sensuous deliberation down the curve of her graceful neck and promised, 'I'm not going to let you go. Just hold on tight.'

Their eyes clashed luminous blue on hot black and she nodded, wanting him so badly that she couldn't articulate the need that flowed through her and made her throat ache with emotion.

There were bands of dark colour etched along the angles of his razor-edged cheekbones as he picked her up and kicked the half-open door with his foot as he strode into the moonlit room beyond.

He pushed aside a pile of cushions, pointless furnishing at any time and right now a damned obstacle, and laid her down on a sofa.

Shining hair spread out around her face, the invitation shining in her luminous eyes, she took his breath away. He wanted her so much that the ache went bone deep, yet still he didn't respond to that invitation. He sat there on the edge of the sofa anticipating but wanting to stretch this moment, glutting his senses on the visual feast.

She looked like every impossible fantasy he had ever had made flesh—warm, soft, inviting flesh.

She shifted, a sinuous feline wriggle of her hips that made the blanket ride higher, revealing another inch of thigh as she held out a hand to him.

He took it and she drew him to her until he lay curved over her, one foot braced on the floor, the other beside her. One hand on the arm rest above her head, the other beside her face, he lowered himself slowly, experiencing a fresh kick of lust as she gasped, her eyes flying wide.

'That is how much I want you.'

The intimate pressure in the soft flesh of her belly, the smouldering intensity in his face sent a rush of scalding heat through her body. 'I want you too.' She did, with a desperation that bordered physical pain.

This was THE MOMENT, the one she had imagined half her life. The one she had begun to think might never arrive, or, worse, might arrive and she might not notice.

Her fears now seemed foolish; this was not something a person could miss.

She was unable to hide her need; her hunger shone in her eyes as she kept her steady gaze trained on his face. Holding his eyes with her own, she reached for the hem of the blanket, arching her body into his as she peeled the blanket from the sofa before lying back down.

Whenever she had imagined this moment Neve had thought she would feel self-conscious, but now it had arrived she felt anything but. The expression of driven need stamped on his dark features as his glance glided slowly down her body did not make her feel insecure, it made her feel gloriously self-assured and womanly.

'*Bellezza mia*, you are...' Severo shook his head; words failing, he stared down at the slim body beneath him. 'You are ravishing,' he said, peeling her light top over her head before thickly reaching for the peak of one breast that strained against her bra.

'I think you're beautiful, the most beautiful man I've ever seen.'

His laugh momentarily eased the tension that drew his strong patrician features taut.

'But you probably already knew that—you seem to know what I'm thinking before I do.'

'I know what you want before you do too, *cara*.' His lean dark face was intent as he peeled back the lacy covering to reveal the smooth curve crowned by a sensitive straining rosy peak.

With a groan he lowered his head and pulled it into his mouth, unclipping the front catch as he did so.

The sensation of his mouth and hands on her, teasing her, stroking her, was indescribable. Grabbing his head, sinking her fingers into his silky black hair, she held him there against her breast.

She writhed beneath him, totally giving herself to the exquisite pleasure of his caresses.

Her hands slid under his robe. She felt him gasp and her hands moved slowly down the strong, powerful, muscled curve of his back. She stroked his skin, marvelling at the satiny texture, revelling at the extraordinary power and strength of his incredible body until he flinched.

Gasping a breathless apology, she belatedly recalled his injury. The thought of his pain made her stomach muscles clench.

'I'm sorry. I hurt you.'

His smoky gaze swept her face. 'If you stop it will hurt more.'

Inside her she felt a deep pulse awake, throbbing with a rhythm that vibrated through her body as she arched her back as he began to tease her sensitised nipples, his hands kneading each breast in turn until finally she begged him to stop.

Severo lifted his head. *'Too much?'* His eyes slid over the sleek supple curves of her delicious body. He did not think he could ever have too much of her.

Her nipples, still damp from his ministrations, tingled as the air hit them. He slid her pants down over her thighs and she lifted her legs and kicked them away, wanting no barriers between them. Without warning he lowered his body onto hers until they lay flesh on flesh.

When she replayed it in her head later Neve identified this as the moment her brain switched off and her instincts kicked in, the moment when everything that was not Severo ceased to exist. For a heartbeat everything stopped, time was suspended, and when it started again she was on fire.

She surrendered totally to the hunger in her veins, hunger that roared like dry tinder caught in the path of a forest fire— Neve was on fire. She gave herself up completely to the heat, responding instinctively to every touch, every caress, kissing him back, touching him.

When he pushed into her with his body she pushed back, nipping at his neck while she reached with shaking hands for the belt of his robe.

Breathing hard, dark bands of colour highlighting the high patrician contours of his cheekbones, Severo rolled onto his back to give her access. Neve, panting as if she had been running, fumbled, her trembling eagerness making her clumsy. Dark features taut with driving need, Severo removed her hand from the folds of his robe and then, holding her gaze took her small hand, separating her fingers and curling them over his erection.

He sucked in a breath hard and gave a hissing sigh as her grip tightened. Then, crushing her to him, trapping her hand between them, he bent his head and kissed her on the lips with hard, bruising pressure, kissing her as if he'd drain her.

She could feel the tremors that shook his powerful body as he continued to kiss her while his own hand moved over her slender curves, caressing her everywhere, making her ache.

It was terrifying and it was marvelous. She was shaking with need as his hand skated across her stomach, then his lips were there, his tongue tracing a wet line over her aching flesh. She twisted sinuously under him, her hands sliding down his sides and along the quivering flanks of his powerful thighs.

He kissed his way back up her body; the leashed power in his body acted like a narcotic on her senses. She couldn't get enough of him. She pushed her face into his neck, tangled her fingers in his hair and pressed her curves into the hard angles of his body as she greedily breathed in the warm male scent of his skin.

As he settled over her she slid her hands over the stubble on the sides of his face and gazed into his eyes, seeing reflected in the dark depths the same hunger that was driving her.

'This feels perfect.'

'It will be,' he promised thickly.

Severo was struggling to retain control; it was a struggle he was losing. He slid his hand between her legs, his fingers touching her hot slickness making her cry out and move restlessly against his hand.

'Please, I can't...this...it's too much...'

His glance travelled from her heaving breasts to her flushed face and without a word he reached for the robe on the floor and pulled a foil packet from the pocket. Then he parted her thighs and, still without a single word, he slid between them.

'Look at me, Neve.'

She did.

He smiled down at her, a fierce smile that made her heart thump. 'Just relax. Remember, just think of me, of this.' Misinterpreting her sudden tension he promised, 'I can make it good for you.'

And he did. He slid into her before she could tense, wrenching a shocked gasp from her parted lips. The pain was fleeting and she was far more focused on the incredible sensation of having him hard and hot inside her, of being filled and stretched by him.

'*Per amor di Dio,*' he breathed, his eyes glittering black as he gazed down into her face. 'You're so hot and incredibly tight.'

When he began to move her dormant instincts that had been waiting for this moment kicked in and she rose to meet him, her back arching, her hands grabbing his sweat-slick shoulders for support as they moved together in perfect harmony, all the time their eyes sealed electric blue on black.

There were no words. Their bodies were communicating on a primal level that eliminated the need for speech. There were sighs and gasps, keening moans of need, but no words, not until the last moment when the explosion inside was peaking and Neve closed her eyes.

'Look at me, *cara*. I want to see. I want to see it in your eyes when you come.'

She responded to the raw urgency in his voice and opened her eyes at the climactic moment of release. Swept away on a tidal wave of throbbing sensation, she was aware of Severo crying her name out as he drove into her hard one last time and then, shuddering, he lay on top of her breathing heavily.

When he rolled off her Neve stared at the ceiling with shining eyes.

She turned her head. 'That was utterly incredible.' She framed his face between her hands and Severo opened his eyes. 'I suppose you know that you're incredibly good at that.' Without waiting for him to reply, she shook her head. 'Of course you do.' She let go of his face and put her head on his chest.

'A man always likes to hear these things.'

'So does a girl. Not that I expect you to tell me I'm the best sex you've ever had, but a well done might be nice.'

This made him laugh until he realised that she was the best sex he had ever had. 'I had no idea I was meant to grade you…next time I will remember.'

She angled a shy look at his face. 'There's going to be a next time?'

'Oh, I think so, don't you?'

CHAPTER NINE

NEVE lay with one arm curved above her head, a contented cat-who-has-had-the-cream smile curving her lips as she emerged from a slow, sensuous kiss.

Even now after they had made love he kissed her like a starving man.

'You know what I'd like now?'

'Give me five minutes…' His glance drifted to her pink-tipped perfect little breasts and he added thoughtfully, 'Or possibly two?'

Her eyes flew open. 'Not that!'

That she could blush after the things they had just shared amused him; her husky laugh made the hairs on his nape stand on end.

'Rejection!' he said, adopting a crestfallen expression. 'And after you told me I was the best—I suppose you say that to all the boys.'

Neve's lashes lowered in a protective sweep and she wondered what his reaction would be if she admitted there were no others. 'Idiot!'

'So what do you want?'

'Food. I'm hungry.'

'You are very demanding.'

Severo raised himself on one elbow, watching as she gave a feline stretch and announced, 'Actually, I'm starving.'

He shook his head and pushed a damp coppery curl from her brow. 'I've never met a woman like you before.'

He would actually have been amazed to learn there was another woman like her. Neve was, he decided, a one-off—unique.

Never met a woman like her before? Slept with, more like.

Wariness drifted across her face, dulling the sparkle of pleasure shining in her eyes.

She had been surprised when he had not appeared to realise that it was her first time. There had seemed to be no reason to explain her embarrassing lack of experience afterwards, but maybe she should? Especially if he was, as his comment suggested, comparing her unfavourably with his previous, obviously more experienced lovers.

Would it make a difference if she told him she was a fast learner?

'What sort of woman is that?' she pressed cautiously.

'One who demands I feed her after sex, but then,' he mused, pulling himself upright, 'I'm not usually around.'

There was a pause before Neve, distracted by the sight of him padding stark naked and totally unselfconscious across the room, responded to the strange comment.

'Not usually around?' With the candlelight making his skin gleam like burnished gold he made her think of a classical Greek statue come to life. She felt her libido stir lazily—he really was utterly magnificent.

'I never spend the night.'

Neve's eyes widened. *'Never!'*

Severo pulled a cold cooked chicken from the fridge. 'Never,' he confirmed, adding, 'Chicken sandwich?'

'Fine.' Neve rolled onto her stomach and, chin resting in her hands, followed him with her eyes. The strange thing was he didn't appear to think he had revealed anything very extraordinary. *'Never?'*

She was no expert, but that seemed more than unusual. Was he a man who had perfected sex but not even reached the learner class where relationships were concerned?

He flashed her a look, puzzled by her prolonged interest in the subject. 'I like my space and I bore easily.'

The casual admission caused the breath to leave her lungs in one gasp. She pulled herself into a sitting position and asked, 'Would you like me to sleep upstairs?'

Planting the plate of sandwiches on a table beside the sofa they occupied, Severo levelled his frowning scrutiny at her face.

'What are you talking about?'

She tossed him a haughty look. 'Well, I wouldn't want to bore you.'

He sat down beside her. 'You're beginning to now,' he lied, unable to imagine this woman ever boring him. Aggravating, provoking and generally driving him crazy, but not boring!

Severo watched as she snatched a sandwich and bit into it, glaring daggers at him as she did.

'Are you going to tell me what I've done or should I guess?'

'Those poor women—how do they put up with you?' The probable answer to that question still shook her body with intermittent after shocks—he not only looked like a god, he made love like one too. 'Wham, bam, thank you, ma—'

The rest of her words were lost in the heat of his mouth.

When his head lifted they were both breathing hard. 'You feel sorry for my lovers?'

She felt *jealous* of his lovers, past and future. Neve stared at him mutely, shocked by the flash of insight she could have done without.

'Or is this about you?'

'How could it be about me? This is a one-night stand.' This little piece of magic would vanish like a dream once the real world intruded. But she didn't want to think about that now.

This was her time, a time to indulge her fantasies free from the normal constraints.

And Severo was definitely her fantasy made flesh—perfect flesh.

'Possibly…'

Neve stared; the intimate ache between her thighs was making her thought processes slow. 'What do you mean "possibly"? How often are we likely to be snowed in together?'

'I don't generally need snow to keep a woman happy in bed.'

The arrogant assertion drew a scornful laugh from Neve. 'My, you really do think a lot of yourself,' she sneered, thinking, I only have a night—why am I spoiling it arguing?

Anger tautened his jaw. 'I have never told lies to get a woman into bed.' And he had never made so much effort to convince one to stay there.

The question was why?

The answer was not complicated: she was the best sex he had ever had.

'I want to spend the night with you.' He did not realise until he spoke how true this was.

Neve stopped chewing.

'Because there's no place else to go?'

He leaned across and brushed a crumb off her chin. 'Because I want to.'

It was enough for him; he did not feel the need to dig deeper—why should she? His glance drifted across her face.

'And I do have six months to make up for.'

And I have a lifetime to make up for, she thought. Cramming a lifetime into one night would take some doing, but she was willing to try. It was strange—hours earlier she had never even thought of herself as a sexual being, now she glowed with the discovery of this essential womanly part of herself.

'That's a lot of making up,' she said, lifting a hand to stroke his cheek.

'One night might not be enough.'

Neve's hand stilled. 'What are you saying?'

What was he saying? 'We could meet afterwards.'

Neve looked away, but not before he had seen the doubt in her eyes.

Having to persuade a woman—he could not even bring himself to think *beg*—was a totally alien experience for him.

Severo did not like it.

'We don't know anything about one another. We might not even live in the same country!'

'So tell me about yourself.'

The instruction made her blink. 'It's really not that sim—'

'I know you have a stepdaughter, so do you have any other family?' Hovering on the outskirts of Severo's thoughts was the knowledge he was actively seeking information he normally avoided.

'Just a brother. Our parents died when I was fourteen.'

'Where do you live?'

'What is this—online dating?' Neve protested.

'It does not matter how much information you feed into a machine, it cannot predict the spark of sexual attraction that draws two people together. Compatibility is not about a postcode, science or a shared love of literature, it is about chemistry.'

Without thinking, she found herself nodding her total agreement.

'I live in London.'

For someone who had just been pretty dismissive about postcodes, he seemed pretty smug about this news. 'I have several homes. One is in London—we are neighbours.' His glance shifted from her face to the depleted plate of sandwiches and back. 'You have eaten enough now?'

She nodded.

Without warning he took hold of her hips and dragged her down the sofa before lowering himself on top of her. 'Finally, I cannot kiss you when your mouth is full.'

It wasn't and he did, then he began to kiss other parts of her and Neve thought she might die from the sheer bliss of it.

When Severo awoke during that half-light time just before dawn he had lost the feeling in one arm. He eased it out carefully from under Neve's body, trying not to disturb her.

She was sleeping like a baby with her head on his chest, her warm body curled up trustingly against him in exactly the same position she had been in when she had fallen asleep a couple of hours earlier.

He looked at her and felt no lessening of the insatiable desire that had driven him last night to make love to her until exhaustion had claimed them both. He had a healthy sexual appetite, but last night had been different. A woman had never aroused him this way or, for that matter, satisfied him as totally—and still he wanted more of her.

She had fallen asleep in his arms but part of him was amazed to see her still there with her hair tumbled around her face and spread out across his body this morning.

But then this was a first for him. Severo had had his share of relationships, but he slept in his own bed and did not warm to the idea of pillow talk.

A person did not want to spoil great sex with conversation and he did not require reassurance concerning his performance.

Last night had been great sex—no, last night had been phenomenal sex! He had never been with a woman who was so natural and passionate, so incredibly…giving? Yes, she gave and held nothing back but asked for nothing in return.

There had been conversation last night and laughter. He knew she had a brother called Charlie who could, if only he found something he really wanted to do, be brilliant. He knew that she was ticklish and she loved milk and dark chocolate but hated the white stuff.

Clenching his hand to speed the return of the circulation to his arm, he shifted his weight slightly and pushed the hair gently from Neve's face, revealing smooth cheeks flushed with sleep.

She murmured something in her sleep and snuggled closer, seeking his body warmth. The heating had switched itself off at some point in the night and not as yet switched on; the room was chilled.

He pulled the rug that had slipped up over her smooth shoulder. He began to stroke her skin, marvelling at the satiny texture as he continued to study her sleeping face.

As his glance drifted to her soft mouth he felt desire sweep through his veins like a narcotic. He was tempted to kiss her awake, but he restrained the impulse; she'd only had a couple of hours' sleep and if she intended to look for the lost step-kid, as she obviously would, she'd need all the rest she could get.

And support too, if the story turned out not to have a happy ending.

Did he offer support? Severo had no idea, this was unfamiliar ground for him, but one thing he was certain about: a one-night stand was not going to satisfy his hunger for her. The problem was he was positive that Neve was not the sort of woman who would be satisfied with his standard formula for a relationship.

She would want more, and not just sleepovers. The question was, was he willing to give it—give that part of himself that he had always held back?

She opened her eyes and he greeted her with a soft, 'Hello, *cara*.'

Big, impossibly blue, they blinked up at him for a moment with total lack of recognition.

Then, as if a light had gone on behind them, the confusion cleared and she smiled at him, the uncomplicated warmth and pleasure in her face taking his breath away.

He was ready. Being on the receiving end of a smile like that was worth a few concessions, and why not? It wasn't as if he were going to ask her to have his children.

'You weren't a dream. I'm so glad.' She stretched, wincing slightly as muscles that had never been used before made their presence felt.

Taking pleasure in her feline grace, Severo reached out and brushed the hair from her eyes. Neve brushed her cheek against his hand and pulled herself up into a sitting position. 'What time is it?'

'Early, still dark.'

She turned her head, saw where his eyes were trained and with an, 'Oh!' slid down under the blanket.

Severo grinned. 'After last night you can blush?' He had explored every delicious inch of her body and she had been equally curious about his; he had delighted in her total lack of inhibitions.

Neve gave a crooked little smile, her brows twitching into a feathery line above her tip-tilted little nose. 'Last night was…' A flush spread across her skin as the memories drifted back. It wasn't just the things she had done—the word wanton sprang to mind—it was the fact that everything had been so natural. When she thought about it now in the cold light of almost-day she still felt a sense of *rightness*. 'Was that really me?'

'Unless you have a twin sister.'

'No sister.'

'Just a brother.'

Neve regarded him in amazement. 'How do you know that?'

'You told me. You were quite talkative at one point.'

She covered her face with her hands. She had had so much adrenaline circulating in her system she'd been high as a kite in the post-coital period. 'Oh, God I must have bored you silly.'

Men, she knew, at least anecdotally, liked to fall asleep afterwards. Now she knew that this did not apply to all men; Severo had not seemed at all sleepy!

'You were many things, but boring was not one of them.' He raised himself on one elbow and took hold of her small hand. 'Last night, I…' He caught sight of the bruise dark against the pale skin on the inner aspect of her wrist and froze.

'What's wrong?' she asked, alarmed by his immobility and the grey tinge under his golden skin.

'Did I do that?' he asked in a stark whisper.

'What?' Neve followed the direction of his gaze, her frown clearing when she saw the bruise. 'Oh, that. It's such a nuisance—I bruise really easily. No, I think I got that one when I smashed your car, so some people might say I deserved it. When you see your car you probably will.'

At the explanation some of the tension slid from his body. 'I was concerned—I have never lost control with a woman before.' She was so damned fragile and small the possibility that he might have hurt her tore him up inside.

She kissed him boldly on the mouth and said, 'You can lose it with me any time you like.' Had last night been just talk or would she see him again?

Channelling bright and breezy, because she really wanted him to carry on believing that she was the sort of cool, sexually experienced woman who took a one-night stand in her stride, she grabbed the wrist he wore his watch on.

'What was the time?' It wasn't as if she had time for a relationship—not until she'd fixed the one she didn't have with her stepdaughter.

He turned his wrist so that she could read the dial.

'I am also glad last night was not just a dream.'

She stilled, wondering if wishful thinking was making her hear something in his voice that wasn't there. She turned her head.

Their glances connected.

It wasn't wishful thinking!

'I think reality is better than dreams.'

She nodded, thinking, This one is.

'At least last night was,' he continued, obviously choosing his words with care. 'However, it still feels…like unfinished business? You agree with what we discussed—that it might be a good idea to continue, pick up where we left off…?'

'A date, you mean…you want to go out with me?'

His grin flashed. 'I was thinking more along the line of staying in with you, but, yes, a date. You need time to think about it.'

Neve laughed. She felt as though all her birthdays had come at once. 'No. Not no, I don't want to,' she corrected hastily. 'I mean no, I definitely don't need any time to think about it.' She rolled onto her side and slid on top of him, loving the feel of his lean, hard body underneath her and feeling a thrill of female power as his erection pressed into the softness of her belly. 'I would really like to stay in with you. Does this mean you're my boyfriend?' Her eyes widened at the rather surreal idea.

With a growl Severo slid a hand around the back of her head and pulled her face down to his. 'If you like.' He slid his free hand over the curve of her bottom, spreading his fingers across the smooth flesh. They didn't have long before it got light and he had no intention of wasting a moment of the precious minutes.

A shiver ran through her as their mouths connected; his kiss was deep and possessive. She returned the pressure, murmuring his name against his lips. The kisses rapidly escalated to wild and their hungry caresses became frantic.

At some point they slid off the sofa onto the floor.

The breath left Neve's body in a soft sighing gasp.

'Are you all right?' Severo asked, levering himself slightly off her.

Neve grabbed him and pulled him back down. 'Fine, don't stop, please don't stop!'

Severo, who doubted he could have stopped even if he'd wanted to, had no problem complying with her throaty plea.

'*Dio mio*, I can't get enough of you!' he growled, flipping her over onto her back. 'But I damned well intend to try,' he panted, sliding a hand between her legs.

A low keening moan emerged from her throat as he ran a finger along her folds until he came to the sensitive nub. She arched under him, biting into his neck.

'Please, Severo, now!' she sobbed, desperate to feel him inside her.

'Put your legs around me, *cara*.'

She looked up at him through a hot haze of passion and did so just as he surged thick and hard into her, driving deep and driving her out of her mind and into her body, aware of every cell and nerve ending as he stretched and filled her.

He carried on kissing her the entire time he moved, stroking into her hard and hot, moving deep, touching the place that ached to be touched by him. Everything was in sync: their bodies, their moans, their gasps and sighs and at the end, their releases.

Afterwards they lay there on the floor, bodies still locked together, panting as their sweat-slick skin cooled. Neve closed her eyes, loving the feel of him heavy on top of her, loving the heat of his breath on her neck, loving the musky smell of his salty skin.

Finally Severo rolled off her, not sure if he was insatiable or insane and not actually caring. 'We will definitely do that again soon.' He was breaking all his own rules and enjoying it.

CHAPTER TEN

NEVE cast one last wistful look at the grey stone walls. She had entered here one woman and was leaving another.

Severo had suggested that they stay put until the rescue services found them, and in truth she had been tempted, but the sun shone from a blue sky on the crisp white snow and she knew that there was no good reason, beyond a strong desire not to delay their return to the real world, not to venture out.

'You left a note?' she checked anxiously as he closed the door.

Severo gave her a look that was tinged with impatience. After the fourth time she had asked him the same question he had stopped counting. 'Yes, I left a note and my phone number along with a promise to pay for any items we used or damage caused. I am the king of courtesy among housebreakers, so relax.'

It was, he knew, a pointless suggestion; he had felt the tension build in her all morning. She was worrying herself sick over her stepdaughter; it was hard not to compare her concern with the utter selfish style of stepmotherhood favoured by Livia.

The snow on the path crunched under her feet as Neve walked up the incline towards what was probably a driveway when it wasn't covered in several feet of snow. Everything, she reflected, gazing around, looked so different in the daylight.

'I'd hate to come home and find someone had been in my home.'

'Careful,' he cautioned sharply as she slipped. Considering the amount of sleep she had had last night she ought to be dead on her feet, but she had hit the floor running this morning and showed no sign of flagging yet.

Actually he felt pretty energised considering the energy he had expended between the sheets—not that there had been sheets, but who needed sheets when he had a soft, warm woman to hold onto and sink into?

He walked behind her watching the gentle swing of her hips while his body sent him a pretty strong message that he still wanted her, though in the cold light of day he was struggling to see her fitting into his life.

He was struggling even more to see her in the role of mistress.

'Accidenti!'

His hand shot out, his fingertips brushing her own as Neve recovered her balance. She flashed him a smile of gratitude for the steadying hand and wondered if the casual contact had sent an electric surge charging along her nerve endings too.

'I'm sure you wouldn't want a stranger to freeze to death on your doorstep.'

'No,' she conceded, thinking, You were a stranger this time yesterday. And now they were lovers… She smiled to herself, liking the sound, but her smile was tinged with caution.

Last night she had allowed herself to be carried along by his determination, flattered and wanting to believe they had some sort of future, but she had never been convinced that the fragile thing that had blossomed in the hothouse atmosphere last night would survive in the real world.

Maybe things were already changing? Last night he had

begun to open up to her, but this morning she sensed that he was regretting some of the things he had said.

She paused to fan her warm face and heard Severo say, 'Exactly. Besides, I'm sure the owners will have more important things to think about when they come home. Slow down,' he added, shadowing her steps, staying close enough to be there to catch her if she slipped.

'What sort of important things?'

Severo was happy to share his theory—at least it took her mind off the missing teenager whom Severo would quite happily have throttled for putting Neve through this sort of hell.

'Did you see those open garage doors?'

Neve nodded. Last night they had approached from the opposite direction and not even known the detached garage block was there.

'And upstairs the nursery full of brand-new stuff.'

'I didn't see that,' she said, wondering where he was going with this.

'It still smelt of wet paint, then there were dates on the calendar in the kitchen pencilled in with antenatal clinic.'

Neve stopped at the top of the incline and turned to face him. 'You think the woman who lives there is pregnant?'

'I think the woman that lives there went into labour during the blizzard. It would explain why they left without turning off lights or locking up. It explains the entire *Marie Celeste* scenario.'

Neve was impressed. 'You got all that from the smell of fresh paint.' A leap but it did fit. 'I hope they reached the hospital,' she said with a worried little frown as she imagined the nightmare journey the couple must have had.

Off the narrow path now, Severo was able to walk beside her as they set off in the direction he was pretty sure the road lay.

'What a thing to happen. Can you imagine how scared you'd be giving birth out in the middle of nowhere?'

'I would be very scared giving birth.' But even more scared to see the woman he loved going through the pain and potential danger of childbirth.

Neve did not respond to the quip. She was thinking about babies; she wanted them one day when she met the right man. 'So would I.'

He gave a disapproving frown and contended, 'You are too young to be thinking of babies.'

His habit of issuing autocratic pronouncements was irritating and had the effect of making her want to say the opposite. 'That's an opinion, but not necessarily mine.'

'I suppose all women are genetically programmed to procreate.'

Neve, who could think of several friends childless from choice who would disagree with that, didn't dispute the claim. 'But not all men?' she asked, flashing a curious look at his patrician profile and wondering if he was actually speaking of himself.

If he was it was a waste because any baby who inherited his genes would be beautiful. She smiled to herself as an image of a dark-haired baby materialised in her head.

'It is different for men. We are designed to impregnate, not nurture.'

He had been anxious to do neither, a fact she was grateful for because, to her shame, it was not something that had crossed her mind, but Severo had been scrupulous about protecting her. Even last night when things had got really wild, then this morning he had…they had fallen…Neve huffed a shocked gasp as the memories of their early morning lovemaking came back.

A look of shock etched on her face, she gulped and walked on.

It seemed that he had not been so scrupulous after all! Not that she was blaming him—the responsibility had been equally her own, and if one slip had any consequences it would be a cruel twist of fate.

'Are you all right?'

Neve turned her head and found Severo studying her face. Her eyes fell from his guiltily.

'Fine.'

He angled a sardonic brow.

'It's nothing,' she said, hoping that time would not make a liar of her.

He continued to look unconvinced.

'I was just wondering...hoping that they were safe, the mother and the baby...' It was only half a lie; she hadn't been thinking about the family, but she was now.

Severo regarded her incredulously. 'It was just an educated guess. There might not even be a family. For all I know they just forgot to switch off the lights when they went to do the supermarket shopping.'

Neve, still frowning, shook her head. 'No, I think you're right.' She brightened as an idea occurred to her. 'We could ring around the hospitals when we get back.'

Severo stared; she was serious! It had obviously not been a good idea to share his theory with her. 'There was dog food in the cupboard—why don't we ring around the animal shelters too?' He made a sound of disbelief in his throat and shook his head. 'Doesn't it get exhausting feeling responsible for everyone, Neve?'

'I'm not some sort of bleeding heart!' she protested indignantly.

The rueful look he sent her was tinged with tenderness that he channelled into irritation; tenderness was a challenging concept for him.

'No, you're a soft heart.' And a soft touch, the sort of person that got taken advantage of, he thought grimly.

Neve, who had been staring fixedly across the snow-covered field ahead, missed the comment. Without warning she began to jump excitedly up and down.

'It's the road! I see the road!' Caution replacing the previous enthusiasm, she turned to Severo and asked anxiously, '*Is* that the road?'

Following the direction of her waving arm, Severo nodded. 'Looks like it,' he confirmed, estimating the distance. 'We should be able to make it in thirty minutes or so.'

They actually made it in twenty because Neve ignored his advice on both pacing herself and caution. She was clearly spent by the time they reached the road, but because she looked so anxious he resisted the temptation to say I told you so.

'So what now?' Neve asked, looking up and down the road that had clearly not received the services of a snowplough.

Reaching the road had been her focus; now she had achieved this objective she didn't feel any closer to finding Hannah.

'We follow it. The only question is north or south.'

'South,' Neve said, pointing to her right.

'That's north.'

She flashed him a look, a reluctant smile curving her mouth upwards as she said, 'I knew that.'

Severo shook his head slowly from side to side. 'You can't admit when you're wrong, can you?'

He managed to keep the distracting banter going for another twenty minutes before Neve's responses grew monosyllabic. He had been conscious that any early success would be heavily reliant on luck from the outset; now it seemed it was dawning on Neve also.

As they progressed and there was still no sign of Hannah, or indeed anyone, he felt her mood shift.

'This is hopeless, isn't it? We're lost. You were right—we should have just waited.'

Seeing her look so despondent broke his heart, but, while he was unwilling to break it any further by agreeing with her analysis of the situation, he was also reluctant to offer her false hope.

'You're tired.'

Neve bowed her head and buried her face in her hands. 'This is all my fault. What if they didn't find her? What if…? This is my fault.'

'I begin to wonder what is not your fault, *cara*.'

'She ran away from me.'

He watched the solitary tear rolling down her cheek and reconsidered his view on false hope; maybe false hope was better than nothing. Maybe not, but the fact was he couldn't bear to see her suffer.

Neve felt his hand on her neck, felt the roughness of the calluses on his palm against her skin as his fingers moved upwards, sliding into her hair and drawing her face into his chest.

It was a moment of sweet calm in the emotional storm, a breathing space. She leaned into him, her arms sliding around his waist as she sighed and turned her face into the hard solidity of his chest, taking comfort from his strength.

'Why assume the worst? Things always look black when you're tired.' Hooking a finger under her chin, he tilted her face up to his. 'And you're exhausted,' he pronounced, swinging her up into his arms and striding out along what was a road when it wasn't covered in several feet of snow.

'You can't carry me,' she protested.

He ignored her and as they continued he was relieved to see her revive like a parched flower given water, and gradually Neve's spirits seemed to lift.

But only temporarily.

Then minutes later her mood went into a downward spiral at the discovery of her car.

'There is no point jumping to conclusions,' he counselled.

Neve swung around on him, her eyes flashing fire in a

paper-white face. 'There's no jumping involved. Look at it!'
Unable to look at the crushed metal, she gave a shudder. 'It's
totally mangled. Are you saying,' she choked, 'that she walked
away from that uninjured?' She shook her head in a negative
motion, sending the Titian curls bouncing across her shoulders. 'I don't think so!' she whispered, closing her eyes.

She sniffed and dragged a hand across her damp face.

'I'm saying, *cara,* that we cannot jump to conclusions.'

Even ones which, in his opinion, were probably correct. It
seemed likely from the extent of the damage that the car had
rolled at least twice before it landed in a snowdrift, where it
now lay almost totally buried. If it hadn't been for the bumper
that he had almost tripped over they might have missed it
entirely.

Neve turned, planting her hands on her hips as she lifted
her face to his. 'So do you think she walked away from the
crash with everything intact and fully functioning?'

Put on the spot this way, what was he meant to say?

'It is possible.'

'I didn't ask you what was possible,' she retorted, her voice
rising as she got angrier. 'I asked you what you thought. You're
not generally afraid to share your opinion. In fact, on the
evidence so far it's hard to stop you! Say something, damn it,'
she gritted, blinking away the tears that started in her eyes.
'Say something!'

'I think the cavalry are here.'

It was not what Neve had been expecting to hear.

'What?'

He pointed and Neve, following the direction of his gesture,
saw a small convoy of vehicles moving slowly towards them. A
snowplough took the lead, behind it was a police Land Rover
and, bringing up the rear, an ambulance.

'Are those police cars?'

Severo nodded.

'Do you think they might know something about Hannah?'

Severo, who thought it was very possible, said, 'We'll soon know.' Very soon the convoy had stopped and the doors were opening.

CHAPTER ELEVEN

It was no surprise that several of the figures who emerged from the vehicles wore uniform. What was less expected was the distinctive blue hair of one who was not in uniform.

Beside him Neve suddenly yelled loudly, 'Hannah! It's Hannah!' And a moment later began to pelt across the snow-covered field towards their rescue party.

The identity of that figure was no longer a mystery.

Smiling to himself, Severo followed, slowing his pace deliberately to give them a few moments alone for what was bound to be an emotional reunion.

As he got closer it was clear that emotions were running high—extremely high!

He saw Neve move in for a hug only to be shoved away by her stepdaughter, who towered a good five inches over her.

'This is all your fault!' the girl yelled. 'If you'd let me go to France with Emma none of this would have happened, but no, *you* had to make me spend the holiday with you because you're only happy when you're making me miserable!' She burst into noisy tears that stopped temporarily when she screamed, 'I really wish you'd died in the snow.'

'Hannah, I'm sorry.'

Severo, who had been standing there willing Neve to do or say something to reprimand her stepdaughter, was stunned.

'Oh, drop the act, why don't you?' the girl jeered. 'They're all on your side now, so you can relax and be yourself—a total bitch!'

Severo's jaw tightened as he watched Neve flinch and bite her quivering lip. He found it totally extraordinary that she made no attempt to remonstrate with the child or even defend herself from the accusations.

'Go on, cry, that'll really get you the sympathy vote,' Hannah sneered.

It was the last straw. The girl had lost her father, but it did not in his eyes excuse her outrageously rude and vicious manner.

Neve was amazed to see Severo walking towards her. The truth was she had fully expected to see him walking in the opposite direction, or even running!

And who could blame him?

She doubted any man expected to meet a girl one day and then be dragged headlong into the middle of an ugly family drama the next!

What was he doing? Neve wondered, watching as he stopped a few feet short of the angry teenager. Hannah, noticing his protective stance beside Neve, rounded on him.

'Ask her—ask her if she ever loved him and see what she says.' She turned back to Neve and screamed, 'If he hadn't been *James Macleod* you wouldn't have looked at Dad twice! Do you think that I didn't always know that you married him for his money? Only you didn't expect to get stuck with me as well, did you?'

Neve, who knew the girl was hitting out in her pain, allowed the accusations to pass over her head, but she could not allow the final quivering claim to pass unchallenged.

'I have never felt I was stuck with you, Hannah,' she said quietly. 'I know what it's like to lose your parents. I just want to be your friend.'

'Friend? Like I'm ever going to be *that* desperate. You were his bit on the side, weren't you? Even when Mum was alive, probably! You think I don't know that you'd have been happy if I'd died last night.'

Neve, sure that not even Hannah believed the ludicrous claim, shook her head and said softly, 'I know you miss your dad, Hannah, but do you think he would—?'

There was no warning as the overwrought teenager reacted. The open-palmed blow scored a direct hit on Neve's right cheek.

'Don't you dare talk about my dad!'

Neve staggered backwards, one hand against her face, the other lifted to stop Severo reacting. She could feel the anger rolling off him in waves.

'Enough. Apologise!'

He did not raise his voice, if anything he lowered it, but his icy tone had a quality that ensured he would be heard.

Neve watched with a sinking heart as Hannah, her face set in a snarling sneer, spun in his direction.

'What's it got to do with—?' Her snarling voice faded, she did a literal double take, her insolent sneer vanishing as she met Severo's eyes.

He angled a dark brow and at his most biting said coldly, 'Well? I am waiting.'

Hannah, visibly struggling to resurrect her defiance, lifted her chin. 'You can wait all you like.' Her show of bravado faded as she met Severo's stare and added with a childish pout, 'I d…don't see what it has to do with you. I don't even know who you are.'

'I am the person who wishes to hear you apologise to the woman who, regardless of the danger, followed you into a blizzard. The woman you struck.'

Tears formed in her eyes. 'She hates me.'

The self-pitying quiver was wasted on Severo, who regarded her with an expression of chilly displeasure. 'It would be no wonder if she did,' he mused, 'because I have to tell you you do not come across as a very loveable young woman.'

'*Severo!*'

At the sound of his name Severo glanced Neve's way.

'That's enough,' she told him.

'No, I do not think it is,' he contradicted, turning back to Hannah. In his judgement a few home truths were overdue. 'In my experience hate does not normally motivate someone to put her own life at risk.'

'She didn't—'

'Yes, she did.' He watched the expression of shocked re-alisation cross the teenager's face and, satisfied he had made his point, continued.

'Your stepmother risked her life trying to save you. And all the thanks she gets is abuse both verbal and physical. Does that seem fair to you?'

'It was her fault—'

Severo lifted his hand to halt the mutinous interruption and Neve was amazed to see Hannah respond meekly to the silencing gesture.

'I am speaking. You will listen. Many people have risked their lives to save you, all because you behave like a spoilt child. I think that instead of flinging the kindness of those who care for you back in their faces you might stop feeling sorry for yourself, take responsibility for your actions and show some gratitude.'

Neve stepped forward, her soft heart twisting in her chest at the sight of Hannah's tears, a pathetic sight that seemed to leave Severo unmoved.

'Severo, *please*,' she hissed in a charged undertone. 'Can't you see she is upset? Leave it—you'll only make things worse...'

'Is that possible?'

Neve was forced to concede he had a point.

'I am waiting.'

To Neve's utter astonishment, after a short pause Hannah glanced her way. 'I'm sorry. I didn't mean any of it to happen.

I just…thanks,' she blurted, adding, 'and I don't really wish you'd died.'

'I'm just glad you're all right.'

She mouthed thank you at Severo before she put her arm around the weeping teenager, who began to weep louder as she leaned down and pressed her face into Neve's shoulder.

Judging that his male presence was superfluous to requirements, Severo moved tactfully away.

A figure in uniform appeared at his shoulder.

'You'll be the couple who took shelter at Coombe Barn? You contacted us last night?'

'Yes.' Severo shook the hand extended to him and introduced himself. 'Severo Constanza.'

'You must be thinking this is a bit of overkill.' The other man laughed, gesturing towards the three nearby parked vehicles.

'The girl got picked up by a farmer who was bringing feed out to stock. I tell you, she is one lucky girl to be walking away from that without a scratch. Her story was a bit—' He shrugged and looked awkward.

'Let's just say we needed to satisfy ourselves that there were no other casualties, so the squad car was actually already on the way here to check out the crash site when they got a report from the chopper crew that two people had been seen walking in this area and one was being carried, which we read as injured, hence the reinforcements.' He angled a questioning look at Severo. 'I'm assuming we were wrong?'

'No injuries.' He did not consider his own scratches fell into that category.

Neve put Hannah in the police car beside a sympathetic policewoman and, promising she would be directly back, hurried over to where Severo stood.

Feeling emotionally drained after the confrontation, she

walked across to where he stood watching; the uniformed man she had seen him talking to earlier had moved away.

She smiled and laid a hand on Severo's arm, her expression apologetic as she said ruefully, 'Sorry about the drama.'

'You have no cause to be sorry.' He touched the red mark on her cheek that had not quite faded. 'Why do you allow that child to treat you that way?'

'It's hard when you lose a parent. You feel angry.' In her case her anger had been aimed at her dead parents; for a long time she had been furious with them for dying and leaving her.

'But why direct that anger at you?' Privately he thought that Neve took tolerance to ludicrous lengths and while she continued to do so the teenager would take advantage.

It was a question that Neve had given some thought.

'Well, even before James died there was some friction,' she admitted. 'And afterwards, well, it's bad enough for anyone to see their name plastered across the tabloids, but for a teenager…' She sighed and shook her head. 'Believe me, school girls are not the kindest creatures on the planet.'

Just one word in the reflective narrative leapt out at Severo. 'Tabloids?' he echoed, a frown pleating his brow.

The interrogative note in his voice made Neve wish she had not introduced the subject at this moment. Maybe she should have told him the story earlier, though she doubted there was actually a *good* time to mention the fact that you were notorious.

'When James died there were some pretty salacious stories—you know the sort of thing, a lot of innuendo and a grain of truth.' Neve kept her voice light; she had determined at the time that she wouldn't allow the horrid episode to make her bitter. 'They decided I was a gold-digging bitch.'

She had hoped he'd see the funny side. His stony expression suggested he didn't, but on the plus side he had not sprung into full protective mode.

Neve had been startled at the way he had waded in to defend her from Hannah. It was nice that he was on her side, but only up to a point. Neve had been looking after herself for a long time and she was not looking for a white knight to fight her battles.

She wanted the man in her life to treat her as an equal.

The silence stretched. When Severo did respond Neve put the oddness in his voice down to exhaustion. Her legs felt like cotton wool and she hadn't carried anyone for miles.

'You are *James Macleod's* widow?' he asked, recalling Hannah's earlier tirade.

She nodded. 'You must be tired—'

'James Macleod.' A nerve along his angular jaw clenched as his glance slid to her burnished head; the scarlet widow, they had called her.

Severo was not in the habit of reading the scandal sheets, but unfortunately for her this was one story he had followed. This one had felt personal, and not just because he had known James. Duped and tricked into marriage by a manipulative, gold-digging younger woman… The story had leapt off the page at him. They could have been writing about his father.

At least Livia had not married a dying man.

Neve had.

The blood throbbed in his temples as he struggled to reconcile the innocent, slightly worried blue eyes raised to his with the manipulative monster whose exploits he had read about.

She had even had a partner in crime: her brother.

'You knew James?'

Something about his stillness worried her, but she felt no warning premonition—not until she saw his eyes.

'I did.'

A sick knot of anxiety in the pit of her stomach, she let her hand fall away from his arm. Something was happening here. She didn't know what it was, but it was not good. Was he still angry about Hannah?

'James did the PR on several projects for me.'

'That's quite a coincidence,' she said cautiously.

'Life is full of coincidences.'

Was it a coincidence, he wondered, that he had nearly fallen into the same trap as his father, or was it a case of genetics? Severo rejected the possibility that he was doomed to repeat the same mistakes as his father.

'Coincidences and family fights.' Her voice was earnest— she wanted him to understand that Hannah was not bad, just hurting—as she added, 'You have to understand about Hannah—'

'I do understand about Hannah.'

How could he not? He had been Hannah, the child nobody had listened to trying to protect the father who had walked willingly to his doom.

And he had taken the first step on that path himself—taken it eagerly. His lips curved in a grimace of self-contempt. She had played the role of innocent stepmother in trouble to perfection and he had swallowed it all.

The worst thing about this situation was that even now, with everything he knew, a part of him wanted this to turn out to be a big mistake! The shameful knowledge filled him with anger, and that anger was directed at the woman who was responsible.

'James was wealthy.'

Shock flashed across her face as she thought, My God, he believes it! Why had she thought he wouldn't? Why had she thought he was different? Why had she slept with him?

And she had been worried that he'd be angry on her behalf. Now that was funny, only Neve did not feel like laughing.

'And, what, thirty years older than you?'

'James,' she said quietly, 'was a lovely man.' Neve was starting to realise how rare a breed that was.

'Did you marry him,' he drawled, 'because he was a "lovely man?" Or because he wrote you blank cheques?'

'It wasn't like that.'

'So he didn't leave you money.' Had she run through it already? Meeting him must have seemed like an opportunity too good to miss. 'Is it true?' he pushed, wanting to see her drop the act if only for a moment and admit her guilt.

She lifted her eyes to his and said in a level tone, 'Is what true?'

It turned out they were right, the people who said that a relationship without trust was doomed. Lucky then, she reflected, that they had not had a relationship—in less than twenty-four hours you couldn't forge a relationship based on anything but attraction.

'Did you know James was dying when you married him?'

She nodded.

'Did he give you money?'

Neve saw the cold condemnation in his eyes and felt her anger stir. My God, she wasn't about to defend herself to this man who had appointed himself her judge.

He was meant to believe in her.

How dared he?

She lifted her chin to a belligerent angle and stared at him directly. 'My relationship with James is none of your business.'

His eyes drifted to the tear running down her smooth cheek; a muscle clenched in his jaw. 'I'd say your relationship with James was very much *a* business.'

Had she seen him as an easy mark too?

'I assume that you were his mistress for some time?'

'You can assume any damn thing you like,' she snarled, thinking he would anyway. 'But you know what I think? I think you *want* me to be the person in those stupid stories.'

His lips curled contemptuously. 'Those "stupid" stories were in every—'

'Oh, sure, and you *always* believe in the journalistic integrity of tabloid journalists—always as in when it suits you, and it suits you now,' she contended, 'because it gives you a way to back away without looking like a total commitment-phobic loser, which, for the record, you are!'

The blood left his face, leaving a greyish tinge to his golden skin and an angry white line around his lips. 'You will not speak to me this way.'

'I will speak to you any damned way I like!' she countered with a determined smile. 'You obviously think every woman you meet is out to drag you to the altar. Well, just so that you know, not this one!' she bellowed hitting her chest with the heel of her hand to illustrate the point. 'You needn't have worried because marriage is the last thing I want. I'm free and I intend to stay that way!'

Without warning, the righteous anger that had made her feel strong and in control left her. Aware that she was moments away from crying, Neve turned, the image of his white, furious face in her head as she began to walk away.

Half expecting him to follow, when she felt a hand on her shoulder she assumed he had.

She spun around, her intention to tell him just where he could put his apology, and found one of the uniformed officers standing there.

Quite quickly into the subsequent conversation the man apologetically introduced the subject of a minor driving without a licence.

Fully anticipating him saying that they were going to prosecute, she almost kissed him when at the end of the conversation he said that they were happy to let Hannah off with a caution.

Neve didn't really know what a caution entailed, but it had to be better than a criminal record and hopefully he was right—it would serve as a wake-up call for Hannah. Not that she was holding her breath.

She could, he offered, travel back in the squad car or the Land Rover. She could see Severo in the Land Rover.

When faced with the choice between spending the journey sitting next to a sulky teenager who hated her and a self-righteous Italian who despised her, Neve chose the teenager—there really was no contest!

When they arrived at the police station—conveniently close, it seemed, to the railway station—she delayed her exit in the hope that Severo would have left.

She thought her wish had been granted until they were crossing the street to the station, Hannah lagging a sulky ten paces behind, when she saw the car, a long low sports car, drive past. Sliding into the passenger seat was the female equivalent of the car—tall, leggy, blonde and incredibly slim, wearing a tiny red dress and long boots.

Holding the door open for her was Severo.

Her heart stopped when she saw him and so did she, in the middle of the road. She was still standing there a moment later when a porter carrying a bag came pelting down the pavement.

'Mrs Constanza…Mrs Constanza.'

She saw Severo turn at the sound of his name, but not his name, *her* name.

Together…same name… She took the slow route but she got there eventually.

Oh, my God, he's married. I slept with a married man and I liked it, actually more than liked it.

Neve wasn't sure who she despised more: herself or him.

She turned, grabbed Hannah's arm and, ignoring her protests, ran in the opposite direction.

'Where are we going?'

'I'll know when we get there.'

It turned out to be a small coffee shop where she sat until she had stopped shaking, on the outside at least.

CHAPTER TWELVE

'NO ONE at the formal will have anything like this,' Hannah announced as she danced her way around the kitchen in the fifties full-skirted prom dress that Neve had brought home for her to try on.

'It fits?'

'It's perfect,' the excited teen enthused. 'And I look beautiful.'

'You do,' Neve agreed, thinking who would have thought a few short weeks ago that Hannah would be talking to her, let alone asking for fashion advice?

A lot of things had happened that a few months ago would have seemed impossible. And you could trace almost all of those things back to one night, a night and a person that together had turned her life upside down!

Even her improved relationship with Hannah, who had taken his lecture very much to heart, could be traced back to Severo, though the trail was not quite as unequivocal as the one that linked him to the really major change in her life.

Neve was pregnant.

Pregnant!

Even with her hand pressed to the suggestion of a bump on her belly, it still seemed totally unreal to her.

But then she hadn't had long to grow used to the idea. She'd had all the textbook symptoms but pregnancy had never crossed her mind, not even for a moment.

Neve wondered if, unable to deal with it at some subconscious level, she had simply blanked the possibility from her mind.

Well, for whatever reason, she definitely hadn't made the connection between the intense tiredness she had been experiencing and a baby. She had put it down to the long hours she had been working since she had returned.

She might still be living in ignorance if it hadn't been for the visit to the doctor. She had gone to ask for something to help her insomnia, and after an examination he had explained that he could not prescribe sleeping pills for a pregnant woman.

She had walked home in a daze. It was later that night that Hannah, arriving home from school for the weekend, had walked in and found Neve sitting on the floor in the bathroom sobbing, after doing a second test in the hope the doctor was wrong.

She had caught on immediately; possibly the blue stick Neve had been clutching in her hand had been the clue.

'God, you're pregnant.'

Neve nodded.

Hannah sat down on the floor beside her. For a long time she didn't say anything at all.

'The father…? The hunky Italian—what's his name?'

Neve nodded. 'Severo Constanza.' Saying his name out loud produced another bout of uncontrollable weeping.

'Does he know?'

'No. I only just know myself.'

'Are you going to tell him?'

It was a question that Neve had been sitting there asking herself. 'Yes…no…I don't know.' Her reply pretty much summed up her level of decisiveness on the subject. 'I wouldn't know where to find him.'

And his wife. Neve had no intention of explaining this minor impediment to happy ever after to her stepdaughter.

Unprotected sex and unplanned pregnancy did not exactly qualify her for the 'perfect role model for a teenager' medal, but put married man into that equation and you added a whole new grubby dimension.

'Men are pigs,' Hannah said matter-of-factly.

Neve had a lot of sympathy for this view, but she made an effort to stay balanced. One rotten—very rotten—apple was no reason to chuck out the entire barrel. 'Not all of them. Your dad wasn't.'

Neve held her breath. She knew it was a gamble mentioning James, but she couldn't avoid the subject for ever.

'True, but Paul Wilkes is. I've liked him for ages, then last week he asked me to the formal, and then he un-asks me because Clare, who said she wouldn't go with him, says she will now.'

'Oh, definitely a pig.' Neve was amazed to find herself sharing a bonding moment with her stepdaughter.

Hannah looked at Neve and grinned; the grin faded as her glance slid to Neve's still-flat stomach. 'A baby...wow!'

The next weekend Hannah came home with a wad of A4 pages covered in print.

She handed them solemnly to Neve. 'What are...?' She stopped as a name on the page leapt out at her. The blood drained from her face.

'I thought you might want to contact him so I put his name in a search engine and it went kind of crazy. It turns out your Italian hunk is this money-making machine. He's famous.'

'All this is about Severo?'

Her stepdaughter laughed. 'God, no, those are just a sample. I'd need a wheelbarrow to carry all the stuff there is on him. People really like to write stuff about him. I think someone has a doctorate in him or some financial system he invented. And he's on a load of committees, charities and stuff like that.'

That had been two weeks ago and so far Neve had not used the information. She supposed she would have to at some point, but the thought of how he might react held her back.

He'd probably accuse her of deliberately getting pregnant. Maybe he already had legitimate offspring—planned offspring.

Severo had been at his desk since six a.m. when his secretary buzzed to say his ten a.m. was still not here. It was fifteen minutes after the hour. He made a conscious effort to control his irritation, aware that recently his temper had been short and his tolerance levels low.

To the point where, if she was to be believed, he stood in danger of losing the best secretary he had ever had—her words, and she was probably right.

Her outburst had been triggered by a simple request to work late.

'No, I won't work late again. You may be married to your job, but I'm not. I'm married to my husband—a very understanding husband who has forgotten what I look like.'

Then the woman he had never even seen look ruffled had burst into tears, which had completely thrown Severo.

After her outburst, clearly over the top, he had admitted to himself that there might be at least a grain of truth in her accusations.

And he needed to do something about it; he needed to vent the unresolved anger that was gnawing away at him.

The problem was he had let Neve walk away acting as though she held the moral high ground. Why hadn't he said or done something?

To Severo the connection with that silence and the volcanic rage he felt building inside was obvious. He could barely function when half his resources were spent holding it in check.

He considered the situation with angry distaste. For a man who prided himself on his control, it was an intolerable

situation—almost as intolerable as waking up every morning
wanting her.

He needed to work the redheaded witch out of his system
for good.

And if that required him to take her to bed for twenty-four
hours it was a sacrifice he was willing to make.

The phone buzzed.

Severo picked it up. 'My ten a.m. has arrived?'

'No, you have a call from a Miss Macleod.'

Severo sucked in a deep breath and expelled it slowly. A
slow smile of predatory anticipation spread across his face.

She had come to him.

'Do you want to take the call?'

'Oh, yes, I want to take the call.'

Severo swivelled his chair so that he faced the window; his
pitch-black eyes glittered as he held the receiver to his ear.
'Hello, *cara*, I was just thinking about you.'

There was a silence before a voice, but not the one he had
been anticipating, echoed down the line. 'I'm not Cara, I'm
Hannah, the one you yelled at. You remember me?'

The anticlimax was intense.

'Hannah, yes, I remember you. How are you?'

'I'm OK, but Neve isn't.'

'She asked you to call me?'

The girl on the other end laughed. 'God, no, she'll kill me
when she finds out,' she predicted gloomily. 'But I didn't know
what else to do. I had to go back to school this morning and
leave her.'

Severo's voice sharpened. 'She is ill?'

'Not ill *exactly*.'

Severo struggled to contain his impatience. 'What does
"not ill exactly" mean?'

'Well, pregnant isn't the same as ill, is it? Though after the
way she was puking when I left this morning it seemed like
ill to me.'

Somewhere inside his skull a man was banging a large hammer. Severo raised his voice above the volume. 'Your stepmother is having a baby?' A mixture of distaste and anger slid through him as he contemplated the man responsible.

Was it possible that she had been pregnant that night they had spent together?

'She's having your baby.'

'She told you this?'

'Uh-huh.'

'I see.' He saw that there were no depths that Neve would not sink to.

'And as you're the dad I thought you should be looking after her. I'm really worried, you know,' she confided. 'She shouldn't be all alone.'

'Relax, Hannah,' he advised. 'I will take care of things.'

Her sigh of relief was audible. 'Thanks for that...thanks a lot. Do you need the address?'

'Yes.' He scribbled down the address she gave on a scrap of paper, repeating it dutifully when requested to do so.

'How pregnant is your stepmother?'

Severo tried to imagine her slender body swollen and couldn't—not when he remembered clearly being able to span her narrow waist with his hands.

He could remember other things but he tried hard not to.

'Three months, of course,' Hannah said, sounding amazed he could not do the maths. 'You know, I was afraid that you'd think I'm making this up.'

'No, I don't think you're making this up,' he soothed. It was not, however, something that he would put past Neve. It was equally possible she was pregnant.

What was not possible was his being the father.

His brain might have deserted him that night, but not to the extent where he had neglected to take obvious basic precautions—though it had been a close thing.

Why the lie when she knew that a simple DNA test would reveal the falsehood?

And why pick him when presumably there were other candidates? The pounding in his temple became a roar as he wondered about the man who had come after him, or even, given the timing, before him.

'Look, I've got a class. Be sure to give Neve my love.'

'I will not forget,' Severo promised grimly.

Five minutes later he walked into his secretary's office. 'Cancel the rest of my appointments for this morning,' he said abruptly. 'Including my ten a.m. if he ever deigns to show up.'

'Will do, boss.'

He turned. 'Make that the day.'

For the next hour Severo paced his office trying to work out what had just happened.

Why had she come up with this preposterous story? Why hadn't she taken the trouble to invent a narrative that was even halfway plausible? Why?

Severo raked a hand through his sable hair, and thought, Too many *whys* and not enough answers—actually zero answers.

But there was always an answer; he knew this. Not perhaps the answer a person wanted to hear, but there was always an answer.

The furrow between his brows deepened as he stared out of the window seeing nothing of the City panorama stretched out below.

He saw a heart-shaped face, big, impossibly blue eyes and a kissable mouth—was she thinking about him?

He shook his head, filled with self-contempt for allowing himself to wonder, a sign of mental indiscipline that equated with weakness in his mind.

Severo had watched his father take back the wife who had

humiliated him on innumerable occasions, and each time he did so it seemed to Severo that his father was diminished, that he was a lesser man than before.

If this was what they called love, Severo had decided at an early age there was no place for it in his life. It was utterly inexplicable to him that his father did not cut his losses and walk away from the destructive relationship. He had enough opportunities—Livia walked often enough, and yet each time when she reappeared, promising it had all been a mistake and things would be different, he took her back.

Looking back now, Severo understood for the first time that his father had never actually believed Livia was about to change. He had just *wanted* to believe—bottom line, he had *needed* to believe.

Severo had been forced to watch, unable to prevent the ritual humiliation his father suffered at the hands of his wife. It didn't matter what the damned woman did, the father he had worshipped always came back for more.

He had been ashamed of his father's weakness, but wasn't avoiding emotional attachment for fear of suffering the same fate a form of weakness too?

Severo pushed away the thought, rejecting it before it was fully formed—the sort of thought that he would not have had before he had encountered Neve.

He pushed for the second time, seeking this time to eradicate the image of her face and the subtle perfume of her body.

Sometimes he thought that when she had stolen his car Neve had stolen his sanity at the same time; certainly she had stolen his peace of mind.

Previous to his meeting her, his life, like his thought processes, had been ordered, the personal and private not overlapping, but neatly compartmentalised. It had been efficient, but lately the boundaries had been crumbling, as had his concentration.

The difference was not in his success—business was booming—it was in his ability to enjoy that success. Achieving a goal had always made him feel more alive, but now he waited for the adrenaline buzz and—nothing!

He picked up a paperweight off his desk and rubbed the smooth stone over the palm of his hand, flexing his fingers and frowning as he replaced it.

The truth in this case was that he had been stupid, but not criminally so. They might never have made it to a bed, but he always had safe sex. Why, even when they had ended up on the floor...

Severo froze, every muscle in his body tense as he tried to remember.

He shook his head. Was it possible?

The futile internal debate went around his head for some time until he exhaled a gusty sigh and reached for the jacket draped over his chair. His jaw set, an expression of resolve in his eyes, he headed for the door.

An unpleasant possibility did not go away when you ignored it. In his experience it gnawed away like acid. No, a man had to face his fears.

CHAPTER THIRTEEN

IT TOOK Sevro an hour to reach the address on the paper.

He drew up beside the pavement in the High Street of the smallish market town, and consulted the scrap of paper.

According to this he would find her at number five. Number five was a small shop that called itself Vintage Inspiration and had a monochrome display of sixties-style dresses in the window.

Had he written down the wrong number? Severo got out of his car. It was possible that the people inside knew where she was.

The old-fashioned bell attached to the door rang loudly when he walked in, his footsteps loud on the polished boards, but despite this nobody appeared.

Severo called out, looked around the deserted shop, with its polished boards, pastel-ice-cream-coloured walls and shelving. The space was not large, but it was attractively and imaginatively laid out to maximise the limited space. He walked towards the desk between the racks of clothes that had, according to the signs on them, been divided into decades, and in some cases eras.

He walked around a mannequin dressed in a pale Victorian slip, delicate and in far from perfect condition, and called out, raising his voice above the soft sound of the Dusty Springfield number playing in the background. His impatience growing when no one appeared, he called out again.

'Hello?'

This time he heard a muffled response, and the echo of hurrying footsteps—hurrying slightly too late if his intentions had been dishonest. The owners, he decided disapprovingly, should review the security or maybe their staff. Anyone could have walked in off the street and cleared out the place.

'Can I help you? I'm sorry to keep you waiting. I was just—' Neve froze, the smile slipping from her face to be replaced by one of almost comical dismay as she identified her neglected customer.

The stack of vintage handbags she was holding slipped from her fingers just as the colour slipped from her face.

She lifted a hand to her literally spinning head, and thought, This isn't happening.

But it was. Impossible as it seemed, Severo was standing in the middle of her little shop looking—her chest lifted in a deep shuddering sigh as a wave of intense longing washed over her—looking more handsome, more virile and actually more everything than any man had the right to look, and also almost as shocked as she felt.

Shocked? But he couldn't be. Fate had not brought him to her door; coincidences didn't come in the shape of six-feet-five lying cheat Italians. He must have known she was here.

And he came looking. Was that a good thing, a bad thing… both?

'Why?'

He ignored her bewildered question and carried on staring at her with an angry fixed intensity that made her want to crawl out of her skin.

'What is this place?'

'A shop.'

A policy of 'say as little as possible' seemed a wise move under the circumstances, and useful—words of more than two syllables were proving taxing for her shell-shocked brain just now.

She saw the spasm of irritation twitch at the sensual line of his lips. The angle of his clean-shaven jaw tightened as he looked around, tipping his head and delivering a silky sarcastic retort in a voice that made the hair on her nape stand on end.

'So this is a shop. I have heard of them.'

Standing there in his beautifully tailored designer suit, he looked elegant and formal and dauntingly in control, nothing like the man she had shared the night and her body with during the blizzard.

He's still the same lying, cheating rat inside, she reminded herself.

'I was just closing.'

His brow knitted into an irritated frown. Then he leaned back against the counter top and smiled. 'Don't let me stop you.'

If he was trying to intimidate her, he was succeeding.

'What are you doing here, Severo?' In her place, her sanctuary. Bad enough he invaded her every waking thought and most of her sleeping ones too—now he was here as well.

There was no escape from the damned man.

She stared at his face hungrily, her eyes running over the arrogant angles and sensual curves and autocratic strong lines. He was a rat but he was still the most beautiful man on the planet!

'What are *you* doing here?' he countered.

The harsh accusation in his voice made her blink. 'Well, Shirley usually does today but she had a dental appointment.' She stopped, the colour climbing to her cheeks. 'You didn't mean that, did you?'

He directed a look of withering disdain at her flustered face. 'Are you trying to be funny?' he asked in a dangerous voice. 'Or merely blurting out the first thing that comes into your head?'

Her thoughts were in such a jumble that she had to think about it. 'The last one.'

'I meant,' he said, adopting the sort of slow voice that some people reserved for children and the hard of hearing, 'what are you doing in this place?'

'Working.' For a clever man he was acting pretty dense. She lifted her chin, pride in her voice as she added, 'It is *my* place.'

Not much by his standards but hers nonetheless, a place that had seemed an impossible dream when she was a teenager.

She had confided her dream to James one day and he had pointed out all dreams were impossible until you went for them.

Conscious of her lack of experience and hoping her boundless enthusiasm would compensate, she had followed his advice. Starting small to test the market, she started up a website selling vintage clothing and accessories. It turned out the demand was huge and the response to her small firm very positive, so positive that six months later she had been able to move and extend the business into this small premises.

'Per amor di Dio!' Severo muttered between clenched teeth. 'I am in no mood for jokes.'

'I'm not joking,' she protested, struggling to think past the knot of longing low in her belly. Looking at him made her insides dissolve. She despised the weakness or flaw or whatever it was in her that made her feel this way.

He was married; she *couldn't* feel this way.

His brows lifted to an incredulous angle. '*You* own this place?'

'Yes.'

He gave a Latin shrug and maintained a mystified expression as he looked around. 'And you make money?'

Neve sketched a smile that left her eyes unfriendly. 'I had totally forgotten the model of tact you are, Severo.' But not forgotten how sensual the curve of his lips was and how looking at it made her insides dissolve.

Then stop looking, Neve!

'Style is not about money, but actually we do pretty well—not by your standards, possibly, but we get by.'

'I was not trying to insult you.' He had intended to establish some sort of rapport before he asked the question, but things were not going as he'd planned.

For starters, finding her in this shop. She had money so why this place...a hobby?

'Not trying,' she echoed, thinking, The same way you didn't *try* and make me fall in love with you, but it happened.

Neve's eyes widened. I've finally admitted it! Talk about denial—I love him!

Oh, God, how obvious was that?

A fractured sigh left her lips. Where was the sense of release facing the truth was meant to bring? The only thing Neve felt was an overwhelming sense of despair and guilt.

She had never believed that you *just* fell in love; there had to be an element of *choice*. Of course you could be attracted to someone, but that wasn't the same.

Falling in love was such an important thing it couldn't, she had thought, be decided on something as arbitrary as sexual attraction.

She had never had much sympathy for people who used falling in love as an excuse for riding roughshod over other people's feelings. Love didn't make a wrong a right.

Well, it didn't, but it made it an awfully attractive wrong.

You couldn't get more wrong than Severo.

Or more attractive.

Watching the colour recede dramatically from her already pale face, Severo took an apprehensive step towards her.

She looked as though she was going to faint.

Pregnant women fainted.

His eyes slid to her belly. She didn't *look* pregnant, though his idea of what twelve weeks pregnant looked like was hazy.

'You should sit down?'

'Are you asking me?'

'It is a suggestion. You look…unwell?'

Her eyes fell from his. The question in his manner was making her uneasy; if she hadn't known it was impossible she might have suspected he already knew. 'I'm fine.'

'Is this really your shop?'

'Why do you have a problem with believing it?' Suddenly she hated him coming here looking down his nose at her shop, judging it, judging her…and most of all she hated him for being the man she loved!

'I don't know why I'm surprised that you're a snob.'

His brows lifted as an expression of astonishment crossed his lean face. 'I am not a snob.'

'Oh, no, you're perfect!' she drawled nastily.

He shook his head and wondered where this burst of aggression had come from—of course, it was well known hormones made pregnant women irrational.

Why not come right out and ask her?

Tuning out the impatient voice in his head, he reminded himself that timing was everything.

'I was merely surprised,' he said, the question waiting to be asked pounding in his skull like a hammer. 'You don't need to work.'

Neve's chin went up. 'I *want* to work.'

His blazing eyes moved across the soft contours of her face. *'I want—'*

The silence that grew was not comfortable; it crackled with tension that made it hard for Neve to breathe. Her heart had slowed to a thud as the blood rushed to her head. She struggled to take her eyes off his face but couldn't; she couldn't stop staring greedily at him. 'What—what do you want?' she whispered hoarsely.

He arched a sardonic brow and said coolly, 'Information.'

The tension evaporated; it had probably not existed outside her fevered imagination.

She folded her arms across her chest, and unfolded them slightly more carefully as the action made her painfully aware of her ultra-sensitive nipples.

'People generally come here for dresses.'

His gaze fell from her mouth, sliding down her slim body still concealed behind the counter; he sucked in air through flared nostrils and gave a sardonic smile.

'I thought I had been sent to the wrong place.'

Neve shook her head in bewilderment, her brow furrowing as she tried to make sense of his cryptic words. 'Sent? Who sent you here? No!' She gave a weary negative shake of her head. 'Forget it, I don't want to know. Just go away, Severo.'

'Is that any way to treat a customer?'

'You're not a customer.'

He walked over to a rail and wheeled it towards her. 'I'll take these,' he said, pulling a wallet from his pocket, then extracting a wad of notes and laying it on the counter.

'I think that will cover it. Now, as a customer will you grant me a little courtesy?'

'Am I meant to be impressed by that childish display?' she asked, producing a childish gesture of her own as she picked up the notes and, tearing them in half, threw them at him. 'I'm choosy about my customers!'

Severo had watched her actions with an expression of total incredulity. '*Per amor di Dio*, woman!' he gritted as he stood there, several hundreds of pounds worth of paper, now useless, scattered on the floor around his feet.

As her breathing slowed she began to share his shock. My God, what had got into her? She didn't do things like that; she didn't snap.

'I'll tape them together,' she said with a shamefaced grimace. She dropped into a crouch and began to pick up the torn notes. 'You made me angry,' she muttered.

With a muttered imprecation he strode over to where she was crouched and, grabbing her arm, pulled her to her feet.

'*Accidenti*, what are you doing?'

Neve smoothed down her skirt, avoiding his astonished stare. 'The money I—'

He dismissed the money with a regal wave of his hand. 'The money is of no importance, though,' he admitted, 'I have never had my generosity flung so literally in my face before.'

Then he completely threw her by throwing back his head and laughing.

His expression sobered as his eyes stilled on her face. 'Are you going to tell me what that was all about?'

'You think you can buy me,' she said, on the defensive; it was pretty hard to defend such childish behaviour.

He released a hissing breath of irritation. 'Why would I seek to buy what I have already enjoyed for free?' He was ashamed of the taunt almost before it left his lips, and would have retracted it had she not reacted quicker.

She reacted to the calculated insult without thinking.

The sound of her hand making contact with the side of his face was shocking.

Staring at the mark on his face, she lifted both hands to her mouth. 'That's terrible. I am so…so sorry.'

He lifted a hand to his cheek and shrugged. 'Let us say that we are quits, *sì*…?'

She couldn't believe that he was taking it so casually.

Heat flickered in the pit of her stomach as she met his eyes.

At that moment someone walked through the door, breaking the spell. Neve turned, recognising a woman who had visited the previous week and gone home with several purchases.

She struggled to gather her shredded composure. A repeat customer was always good news, especially one whose arrival was so opportune.

Neve gave a manically cheerful smile. 'Hello again. If there's anything I can help you with, just sing out.'

The woman said, 'Well, actually, my daughter is going to a twenties party next month and I was wondering if—'

'I've had this marvellous flapper dress in the back, not perfect condition, but—'

Severo's snarled oath swung both women's attention in his direction.

'Just one sec.' Neve smiled apologetically at the customer before turning back to Severo, directing her gaze at a safe point over his left shoulder before she said with frigid formality. 'I'm sorry I couldn't help you, sir.'

Severo began to walk towards the door. For a split second it seemed that against the odds he had actually taken the hint. He opened the door but instead of going through it, stood to one side and said to the customer, 'We are closed.'

Of all the cheek! 'We are not closed!'

'This is personal, you understand.'

The woman who had looked initially confused looked from Severo to a flush-faced, angry Neve and said, *'Oh.'* And, with a knowing smile, walked towards the door, promising to be back later.

Neve watched, her mouth ajar with disbelief as Severo closed the door behind her and locked it. 'Now we will not be interrupted.'

Neve planted her hands on her hips. 'How dare you?'

He looked mildly surprised by her reaction. 'You wish to discuss our private business in front of strangers?' He gave a fluid Latin shrug that made her oversensitive stomach muscles flip. 'It is fine by me, you understand, but I assumed—'

'You're a stranger.'

'Do you say that to all the men you spend the night with? Or am I special?'

Neve ignored the question and eyed him with suspicion and dislike. 'What private business?'

'I have been told some things that I need confirmed or denied and I am not leaving until you have done so.'

Neve reminded herself that there was no way, short of bugging her bathroom, that he could know.

'Do you have to make everything sound like a threat? Not everyone responds well to bully-boy tactics, you know.'

A look of utter astonishment crossed his lean face. 'You are calling me a bully?'

She pursed her lips and refused to retract the statement even though she knew it was a slight exaggeration. 'Look, say what you came to say and go.'

'Is there somewhere private?'

'You made this private,' she reminded him bitterly, waving at the locked door.

'Are you pregnant?' He had walked in knowing what reply he wanted to hear; between then and now his attitude had shifted into a grey area—pale grey. He was veering towards the yes camp.

Not as irrational as it sounded. He would one day need an heir—why not this child?

Neve was totally unprepared for the blunt question.

He looked equally unprepared for her reply.

'Yes.'

'And it is mine?'

She nodded. In none of the many versions of this scene she had played in her head did he respond to the news with such a total lack of emotion.

'Perhaps we should go into the back.' Where there was a chair to sit down on before her shaking knees gave way.

Severo followed her into the back room, a small room made smaller by his large presence. To say it was furnished simply was being generous. There was a saggy armchair, a kettle, two mugs and a radio on the small coffee table. Right now it also held the boxes of new stock she had been taking from the back of her car when she had rushed out to serve a customer.

A customer that had turned out to be Severo. It was academic now, but she couldn't help but wonder how on earth he had known—nobody knew except... She stopped dead, a sudden suspicion gripping her.

Before she could demand confirmation of her suspicions Severo spoke.

'You are sure of this?'

Angry colour rushed to Neve's cheeks, though really she couldn't actually blame him for looking for a get-out. What man wouldn't? 'Luckily I was having a slow month so, yes, I know you're the father.'

He gave an impatient scowl. 'I simply meant were you sure about the pregnancy. I accept that I am the father if you say so.'

He had assumed that she had planted the idea of contacting him in Hannah's head, but nobody could feign the sort of shock she had shown when he'd asked if she was pregnant. The expression in her eyes had not said clever scam gone wrong, it had shrieked dismay and confusion.

Neve, aware she'd jumped the gun again—but at least this time she hadn't waded in with the left hook—gave a shamed grimace and said without thinking, 'You took precautions.'

Left to her the pregnancy would not have been accidental, it would have been inevitable! She had not only abandoned her moral principles that night, she had abandoned common sense too.

'Look,' she added with a sigh. 'I know that this is my fault, and you needn't worry, I'm not going to ask for anything from you,' she promised him earnestly. 'There's no need for anyone else to know.' Was he worried that his marriage would be in danger if his wife found out?

Severo looked at her as though she had gone mad. '*I needn't worry?*' He shook his head and began to pace up and down.

The oddness in his voice made her frown. 'Well, biologically you're the father, but I chose to keep this baby.'

The colour seeped out under his tan as he dragged a hand through his dark hair and slowly turned to face her. 'Is that why you didn't tell me?'

Her eyes fell from his. 'I was going to tell you at some point.' She just hadn't decided what point.

'You thought that I would pressure you to end the pregnancy?'

'No, yes...' She shrugged; it had crossed her mind. "Well, it was possible and I didn't want to argue. I've not been feeling great and—'

He snarled something in his native tongue—you didn't have to be bilingual to know it was probably unrepeatable. He looked angrier than she had ever seen him.

'Life is precious!' he bellowed.

'Don't yell at me!' she said, almost matching him for decibels. 'You're preaching to the converted. I just thought, well, it's not as if you'll be able to have much contact with the baby—not unless your wife is *very* understanding.'

Severo frowned. 'Wife? What wife?'

Neve's lips tightened in disgust. 'Please, Severo,' she begged with an attitude of weary distaste. 'Nobody likes to be caught out in a lie. But what's the point denying it? I saw you with her.'

'I have no wife.'

She was bewildered by his attitude; he acted as if saying something didn't exist made it vanish.

'I have never been married, or engaged or even in a long-term relationship. I don't know who or what you thought you saw, but it was not my wife.'

Neve felt a flicker of uncertainty. 'I saw you at the station—you were in a car with a beautiful blonde, tall, long legs...' She stopped as she saw recognition flash across his face, swiftly followed by revulsion.

'Livia?' He spat the word out like a bad taste. There was no way such repugnance could be feigned. 'You thought Livia was my wife!'

'The porter, he called her Mrs Constanza,' she protested.

'She is. Livia was my father's wife, my stepmother.'

Not his wife...not his wife.

'I cannot believe that you thought I was married to Livia!'

It was hard not to wonder about his obvious dislike for the woman his father had married. Actually dislike seemed too mild a word for his feelings. 'She's very beautiful and young—'

CHAPTER FOURTEEN

'BEAUTIFUL!' Severo gave a scornful laugh. 'She has had so much surgery I doubt if even she knows which parts of her body are originals. She is vain, utterly self-obsessed and she wouldn't know a moral if she fell over it.'

He stared at Neve and thought, And how did I ever think you were like her?

'I take it you're not close.'

'The woman killed my father long before he died. She had a series of affairs, and she was not discreet, and each time she came crawling back my father forgave her. I used to despise him for believing her promises. Now I see that he did not, he just pretended to because she was like a drug for him.'

The woman he described sounded more like a disease to Neve.

'It must have been awful for you watching...?' Neve got an emotional lump in her throat the size of a boulder just thinking about how awful it must have been for Severo witnessing this destructive relationship.

No wonder he had never married—what he had seen was enough to put anyone off the institution.

'I'm sorry, but when I saw you with her I thought...'

Severo summed up her thoughts in one sentence. 'You thought I lied to get you in bed.' He would have he still might.

She nodded.

'That perhaps explains the slap.' He lifted his hand to his face and the flush on her own cheek deepened. 'You thought I lied, but you *did* lie when I arrived, didn't you, Neve?' he said quietly. 'A lie by omission, but a lie nonetheless.'

'I didn't tell you but you knew.' She gave a baffled shake of her head. 'How?'

'I had a phone call from your stepdaughter this morning. She was very anxious that I accept my responsibilities.'

Neve's eyes flew wide. 'Hannah! But why would she do that?'

'She was clearly concerned about leaving you alone.' And he could see why.

Neve looked about as far removed as was possible to imagine from the manipulative man-eating monster he had come to confront. It was an image, he realized, that he had built up in his head, an image that bore little resemblance to reality and one that had crumbled away the moment he'd laid eyes on her.

He recalled her angry accusation—what had she said? He wanted to believe the stories because he was running scared, looking for an excuse.

At the time he had dismissed it out of hand, but wasn't there, he wondered uneasily, an element of truth in the accusation?

He prided himself on being objective so why had he not even entertained the possibility that she might be innocent of the crimes?

Why had he refused to believe the much more plausible possibility that she might be an innocent victim of a media witch-hunt?

'I told Hannah I was fine and I am.'

Severo gave a laugh. 'Have you looked in the mirror?' The sooner he had her under his roof and was able to take care of her, the better, he thought, applying his considerable intellect to the easiest way of bringing this about.

Neve gave a tight smile. It was always an ego-enhancing experience to be told you looked a wreck by a gorgeous man.

'So you two are no longer fighting?'

'No. It's good—we've bonded. It's a sisterhood thing—we both hate men.'

Her flippancy drew a tight smile that did not reach his fabulous eyes. 'With no exceptions?'

'We have strict criteria for the good guy pile but so few make it.'

Severo did not bother asking what pile he had been placed on, but he suspected he came somewhere below serial killers.

'I will put things in motion this afternoon if you let me know what dates suit you.'

'Dates for what?'

'The wedding. I don't know if you have any religious affiliations?'

Neve shook her head. 'Hold on, back up there—marriage? What are you talking about?'

'You are having my baby. What is there to talk about? I am not a man who avoids my responsibilities,' he told her sombrely.

Neve chewed her lip. Had it not occurred to him that she didn't want to be a responsibility?

'I appreciate the sentiment but I've done the convenient marriage thing once and, while I don't regret it, this time I'm not prepared to settle—I want the real deal.'

'Settle?' he echoed. 'You think marriage to me would be settling?'

'I'm sorry if that offends you.' And it clearly did.

'I do not think you are sorry. I think you go out of your way,' he contended furiously, 'to do just that!'

'Don't be ridiculous.'

'There are women who would not think being married to a man who can afford to indulge their every whim *settling*.'

'Maybe I'm holding out for someone richer? Or maybe… maybe,' she yelled, glaring up at him, 'maybe I'm not a gold-digging tart you can buy. Maybe I'm not a problem you can just throw money at and walk away.'

He regarded her with baffled frustration. 'I am not trying to buy you. I am trying to take care of you.'

'I can take care of me and Hannah and this baby. When I marry it will be to a man who understands what love is.'

Severo, who had gone white, flinched as she flung the last word at him like a missile.

'You will marry me.' Neve took an involuntary step backwards; he was literally vibrating with anger.

'Because,' he continued in the same low, impassioned voice, 'I believe you know that a child needs two parents. And you know that a part of being a parent is putting your child's needs ahead of your own.'

'So if I don't marry you I'm being selfish—nice guilt trip, thanks. This is the twenty-first century. There is no stigma attached to being a single mother. A woman does not marry someone because she is pregnant, especially if he's the first man she ever slept with.'

Maybe he wouldn't notice her slip?

'First man you ever slept with?'

Neve expelled a gusty sigh; so he had noticed.

'I,' he said, breathing hard, 'was the first man you slept with?' His lustrous dark stare glittered as his eyes moved across her face. 'You were a virgin?'

She nodded and heard the breath leave his lungs on one shaky gasp.

'How,' he asked, looking stunned, 'is that possible?' In his mind a virgin was shy and required coaxing. Neve had been wild and totally uninhibited. Then he recalled the tightness and her little gasp and he closed his eyes, his face like that of a carved bronzed statue. He was submerged by a wave of guilt as he recalled the unrestrained way he had made love.

'I know. I always felt a bit freaky,' she confessed, growing concerned by his silence and odd manner.

'"Freaky?"' he echoed in a choked voice.

'I didn't plan it that way. It just sort of never happened,' she said, thinking, *You* never happened. 'I was never very…highly sexed and, well, my marriage to James was never anything but a paper thing. He wanted someone he could trust to look after Hannah when he was gone and how could I say no? He could have sent Charlie to prison when he stole that money.'

'*Stop!*' he pleaded, holding up his hand to stem the flood of detail.

It took Severo several minutes of patient questioning and prompting before he got the full picture. It was one of a child who from an early age had been expected to care for, not just herself, but others.

And I thought I had a tough time! Now, just as she had her first sniff of freedom, he was perpetuating that cycle—he had got her pregnant.

He felt like a total bastard. No wonder she had looked ready to bolt when he had proposed!

A virgin…? *Dio*, that was the part that he struggled with most, how any one so warm and giving and… The how aside, he could not regret it, Severo decided, even if that did make him the bastard she obviously considered him to be.

Obviously he was genuinely appalled by the possibility he might have hurt her, but at the same time aroused more than he would have imagined possible by the knowledge that he had been her only lover, and now she was carrying his child.

The knowledge spurred him into action.

'Pack your bags. You are coming with me.'

'I beg your pardon?'

His scorching eyes swept her face. 'I am not leaving you here alone. Who else is going to look after you? This brother who gambles and leaves you to feed and take care of yourself?'

'Charlie has had his problems but he's turned things around and Lucy has really been a good influence. He's got a steady job and—'

'Fine...fine... I'm sure your brother is a model citizen and you might well be able to take care of yourself, but Hannah does not think that.'

'Hannah? What has this got to do with Hannah?'

'You had the burden of responsibility heaped on your shoulders when you should have been enjoying yourself. Do you want the same thing for Hannah?'

The suggestion appalled Neve. 'Of course not!'

'Then come with me. My home is large—you need never see me if you don't wish to, but the gesture will cost you nothing. Hannah can come and stay at weekends.'

At least he had stopped talking weddings. 'I suppose...' she began slowly. 'For a while if Hannah—'

'Excellent! I will help you pack.'

'I can pack by myself.'

If Neve had any doubts about the choice she made, Hannah's reaction to the news made her realise that she had made the right decision.

'Whew, that is fantastic. You have no idea how worried I was, and that means I can go on that trip to Bruges next weekend. You're all right with that, aren't you?'

She reached the hall of the flat, where he waited, with her case in her hand.

'You have told Hannah our news?' he said, taking the case from her hand.

'All right, I admit it—you were right.' And Neve was annoyed with herself for not realising what had been obvious to him. 'Hannah won't be coming home this weekend. She's going on a school trip.'

To his credit Severo did not rub salt in the wound, and,

once she had been established in his luxurious London home, true to his word she had all the privacy and peace she could have wanted. A fact that did not delight her nearly as much as it should have.

In fact she had still been unpacking when he had boarded the private jet that was carrying him to some vitally important meeting or other. Clearly it was business as usual as far as he was concerned, but to what extent? Was he willing to make any compromises to his lifestyle? This was a subject Neve knew she had to raise when he returned... It was not a conversation she was looking forward to.

I'd prefer you didn't bring your girlfriends home while I'm living here.

Neve used his absence to acclimatise herself to new surroundings. The household was run like clockwork by the army of staff, who treated her with polite deference. She couldn't wait to escape her luxurious cage to go to the shop, where she only casually mentioned her change of address.

On the second evening she discovered the leisure suite in the basement of the Georgian town house. The following evening her gentle laps of the pool coincided with Severo's explosive return.

Neve was in the middle of the pool when the peace was shattered by the sound of the door hitting the wall and, as she later learnt, several glass panels cracking.

Treading water, she watched as the figure in the impeccably tailored business suit strode to the edge of the pool and threw a large bunch of flowers at her.

She looked from the petals floating on the water to the man who stood there vibrating rage and heard herself say calmly, 'Are they for me?'

'You know they are for you,' he gritted, taking the card from his pocket and reading out loud.

'"To Neve, my one and only true love, all the best, and congrats, Chaz."'

Neve swam slowly to the side. Once there she raised a hand. There was a pause before he reached down, grabbed her wrist and hauled her up onto the side.

The display of strength made her stomach muscles flip in response.

His eyes slid down her body and control slipped several more notches. The sight of the water streaming off her lush body was just about the most erotic thing he had ever seen; he wanted her here and now.

'So?' Severo challenged, pinning her with a smouldering stare.

She shrugged, smiled gently and lifted her shoulders. *'So?'*

Severo swore under his breath. 'Who is this Chaz who sends you flowers to my home?'

'Chaz is Charlie, my brother. I wrote to tell him about the baby.'

The silence stretched.

'Were you jealous, Severo?'

A muscle clenched along his jaw. 'My father turned a blind eye to Livia's infidelities... I am not my father.'

'And I, Severo, am not Livia.'

The understanding in her blue eyes made him swear and swing away.

Later that same evening Neve sat in the panelled dining room at one end of a twenty-foot-long table that glittered with crystal and silver. The place opposite her was laid but remained untouched, and the extra care she had taken with her appearance similarly unadmired.

Neve had lain in bed, her body as stiff as a poker, for half an hour before she sat bolt upright.

'This,' she announced to the silent room, 'is stupid.' She could wait for ever and he was not going to walk through that door saying, I love you more than life itself.

She had to deal with reality, Neve told herself, and the

reality was she was lying here wanting him and a few doors away he was lying there wanting her. Oh, please let him be wanting me!

Someone had to make the first move and open those doors.

Pulling on a floor-length silk robe—she had been sleeping in the buff—she tied it firmly around her waist—she still had one—then walked along the silent corridors to the suite of rooms she knew Severo occupied.

She lifted her hand to knock on the door and stopped. Lifting her chin she boldly opened the door and walked in.

The room was in darkness; she could see shapes but not definition.

Neve swallowed, suddenly feeling a lot less certain this was a good idea.

'Are you lost?'

The sound of his voice made her stomach flip.

'No.'

She blinked as a light was switched on revealing Severo sitting upright in the big four-poster.

He appeared to be wearing less than she was, which was not a lot. Without a word he folded back the cover beside him, the gesture not nearly as articulate as the one that gleamed in his eyes.

The breath snagging in her throat, Neve glided towards him, only stopping when her thighs made contact with the wooden frame of the bed.

Lifting her chin, she slipped the loop of the belt that tied her robe and let it slide from her shoulders. All the while Severo's eyes did not leave her face.

'You are lonely, *cara*.'

Neve bit her lip. 'You have no idea,' she whispered.

'Oh, I think I might,' he said, reaching for her. His hand went to her belly. 'The baby—it is all right for us to—?'

Neve held his hand where it was; his awkwardness made her smile. 'It is all right,' she confirmed softly.

He drew her to him, cupping her face in his hand to tilt it up to him. 'I have not asked how you feel about the baby.'

She was not prepared for the question, and Neve's eyes fell from his. 'How can I feel? It's happening…'

'You're avoiding the question so I assume that you are not… happy.' Did you expect her to be? 'I know this is something that we did not plan, but in time you—'

Neve cut across him as the fears she had been afraid to admit even to herself came rushing out. 'It's not the baby, it's *me*… I mean, my parenting skills with Hannah weren't exactly dazzling… What if I make a terrible mother?'

Her composure crumbled as he drew her shaking body into the shelter of his arms.

His expression was tender as he kissed first one eyelid and then the next before he drew her face into his shoulder. 'You will be a marvellous mother,' he said, stroking her hair.

Her teary face lifted. 'You really think so?'

'I know so,' he said firmly. 'All a child needs is to know they are loved. The rest…we will learn…and I know, *cara*, that you are a fast learner.'

'And you are a pretty good teacher.'

The shy invitation shining in her eyes took his breath away.

Severo was shaking as hard as she was as he rolled her beneath him. The raw, leashed power in his body excited Neve more than she would have thought possible.

'This time,' he promised, 'it will be special and I will not hurt you.'

'It was special the other times too,' she whispered. 'And you never hurt me.'

But he did make her cry, though not until the next morning when she returned to her room to find it full of flowers. Every surface was crammed; they were everywhere, filling the air with their sweet perfume.

Flowers but no note—Neve allowed herself to hope that actions spoke louder than words.

CHAPTER FIFTEEN

NEVE felt the phone in her pocket vibrate and put down the boxes she was bringing in from the car, thinking if Severo saw her he would insist on a private bodyguard to save her from herself.

He was proving to be ridiculously protective, but also, much to her surprise, rather good at practical things like holding her head when she was throwing up.

She gave a distracted smile to a passer-by as she fished the ringing phone from her pocket.

'Neve, have you seen it?' Hannah sounded scared.

'Seen what?'

'The headline in the paper.'

'Which paper?'

'All of them, I should think,' Hannah replied. 'And you obviously haven't, because if you had you'd know exactly what I'm talking about.'

The phone wedged against her shoulder, Neve continued to listen while she eased the box towards the shop door with her foot as she started to open the door with her elbow.

'Severo—'

Neve let the door close, two bright spots of colour appearing on her cheeks as, her voice sharp with anxiety, she asked, 'What's wrong with Severo?'

There had been nothing wrong with him when he had left her bed that morning.

'There are stories all over the papers about him.'

For the duration of Hannah's dramatic pause Neve's mind produced several possible reasons Severo might be in the headlines, including rumours of a romance with some model or long-stemmed aristocratic beauty, or—

'They say he's lost all his money.'

Neve, waiting for the punchline, after a few moments realised there was none.

'Severo?' She shook her head from side to side as she leaned back against the shop window, blocking the window display. 'That's not possible,' she said positively.

'That's what some of the pundits say too,' Hannah admitted. 'They can't associate failure with Severo Constanza, but a lot of others are saying there's no smoke without fire.'

Neve's hands clenched into tight fists as her temper spurted. 'You mean this is just a rumour…gossip.' Even if it was she knew that gossip could be destructive; gossip could destroy reputations.

'Hey, don't get mad with me. I didn't write the stuff, I just bought the newspaper. Since he asked you to marry him I figured you had a right to know.'

'Oh, my God, how must Severo be feeling?' She blew her nose noisily and added, 'He'll be totally devastated. His work is his life, Hannah. And he won't pass the buck, he'll take all the blame. He's got a really overdeveloped sense of responsibility.' Which was why he had proposed.

It would kill him to be forced to ask for help, and how many would want to help now? Tight pain swelled in her chest as she thought of him being alone.

Damn the man. If anyone did try he'd push them away because he'd never admit he needed anyone. Of course, he would come back—that was a given. She had total confidence that Severo could do anything he wanted to if he set his mind to it, but in the meantime…? Neve lifted her chin. She might not be able to offer much in the way of practical help, but she could be there to do what she could.

'I'll speak to you later, Hannah, and don't worry!' she yelled, sliding the phone back into her pocket as she opened the door and yelled, 'Could you put this box in the back, Shirley, and lock up when you leave? Something's come up.'

Fifteen minutes later she was stuck at a red light when she had her inspired thought.

She might after all be able to offer more than moral support. She had almost forgotten she had money.

'I'm rich!' she shouted cheerfully.

The question was how rich?

A slight detour took her to the office of the solicitors who had dealt with James's estate. When she requested an interview and stressed the urgency she was seen straight away.

Refusing the polite offer of tea and biscuits, Neve got straight to the point.

'The money James left me—how much exactly is there?'

After the will had been read Neve had been quite clear: she wanted nothing to do with the money; as far as she was concerned it was not hers. She had explained to the solicitor it could stay where it was or, better still, be given to charity.

The worried solicitor had earnestly begged that she make no hasty decisions, stressing that the decision was hers, but suggesting she gave just ten per cent of the total to charity and then reviewed the situation in twelve months' time.

'You might think differently about it then.'

He'd been right.

'Including the property in France and the...let me see...'

He mentioned a sum that made Neve's jaw drop.

'I had no idea,' she admitted with a shaky smile. 'So how much of that is cash?'

'You're thinking of buying something?'

'More making an investment. Do you think you could put some figures on paper for me?'

'Will Monday be all right for you, Mrs—'

'I was thinking sooner—actually more like now.'

An hour later Neve, armed with the information she needed, parked outside the towering Constanza building and approached the big glass foyer with a mixture of trepidation and determination, pausing only to shout, 'Vultures!' at the news crew filming there.

The conversation returned to the question that perplexed everyone assembled for the strategy meeting.

'I just don't understand where this story of a financial crisis started? I mean, there is no crisis, or at least there wasn't.'

Severo leaned back in his seat as the subject was discussed once more around the table; he knew exactly where it had started. It had started, unless he was mistaken, with his impatience and a throwaway comment.

It had been bad timing. Livia had turned up at totally the wrong moment and in an attempt to get rid of her—he should have gone for the throttling option—he had sent her on her way with the terse advice to 'find another banker, this coffer has run dry'.

He had then forgotten the conversation—he had a lot more on his mind—until he picked up the financial pages this morning. He should have known better. Livia had always been a very literal woman, but practical too. In the same paper was the announcement of her engagement to a banker, a middle-aged man who, to Severo's knowledge, had already run through four wives. It had the hallmarks of a match made in heaven.

'A source "close to the family", this paper says.'

Severo placed the pen he had been threading through his long fingers down on the blotter and responded to the questioning looks flashed in his direction with a shrug.

'The market is really nervous,' his head of development said gloomily.

'The market is not nervous,' a colleague contradicted with equal gloom. 'It is terrified. We have to make a statement to stop this speculation.'

There was a general murmur of assent around the table.

Only one voice was raised in disagreement.

At first inclined to be amused by the conversation, Severo was becoming irritated by the growing level of hysteria in the room. Generally he encouraged debate and a bit of healthy dissent, but this debate was not healthy.

The bottom line was his senior management team could discuss and debate all day but, in the end, the final say was his. They could and probably would be unhappy about his decision, but they were not in a position to challenge it.

'We do nothing. We do not deny or confirm, we just continue business as usual,' he announced to his horrified audience.

Severo could multitask, but on this occasion he chose not to. All his attention was needed to focus on making Neve see sense.

And besides, his instincts told him that it would be a mistake to enter into a dialogue. Doing so would only grant the stories circulating a degree of credibility.

As he was by nature proactive, he found it frustrating to step back and let things follow a natural course. But this was one occasion when no action was the best action.

Other situations required a more hands-on approach. Giving Neve breathing space to reach the right conclusion had been a mistake. For starters there was no guarantee that she would make the right choice and that was not a risk he was willing to take; that was not a situation that required he sit back and wait for events to unfold.

It was time to take charge and force the pace.

'I know, Andrew, how much has been wiped off the value

KIM LAWRENCE 171

of the company, but when the market settles, which it will, when the hysteria dies a natural death, which it will, we will recover the losses. This company is not a house of cards. It can withstand this temporary blip. Now, if you'll excuse me I have more urgent—' Severo came to an abrupt halt. *More urgent?*

He understood the shocked looks of disbelief on the faces of his senior management team. A short time ago nothing would have been more urgent to him than the smooth and successful running of this company.

It mattered to him, of course it did, but Severo realised that his index of urgency and priorities had undergone a seismic shift over the past few months. Now what was urgent, what was vital to him, was having the woman who carried his child at his side, not just for the odd night, but permanently as his wife.

He would ask her again tonight.

What if she wouldn't see sense? The uncharacteristic negative thought surfaced unbidden in his head. Even more uncharacteristic was the sharp shaft of immobilising panic, a deep dread that followed close in its wake.

Severo's jaw grew taut as he pushed through the dread. It wasn't going to happen because he wouldn't allow it to happen. When he set a goal he went for it, not stopping until he had achieved his objective. Some people called it ruthless; he called it focus.

Success had always been the ultimate goal for Severo, a reward in itself. And when he got bored he simply applied himself to a bigger challenge. If they called the challenge impossible, all the better—it simply added spice.

Now that challenge had stopped being enough.

When did that happen?

Now he wanted what he had always previously actively avoided.

This was not a sign of weakness; the ability to change was

necessary to survival. He was, he told himself, adapting to the altered situation.

What man would not want to see his child born and grow? What man would not want to share his successes with the woman he— A shell-shocked expression on his white face, Severo pushed his chair away and rose to his feet.

The men sitting around the table watched with consternation as he walked out of the room without another word.

He had been sitting alone in his office for thirty minutes when his secretary buzzed through.

'There is a Mrs Macleod to see you. I told her you were not available but she—'

Severo cut across her. 'Send her in.'

Neve was wearing an individual combination, even for her—an orange cardigan and a skirt with red tulips on. Severo did not notice the clashing colours, but he did notice the scent of roses that entered the room with her; he noticed the creamy tint of her bare face, the soft flush on her cheeks and the pinkness of her lips.

Seeing her face satisfied an unacknowledged hunger and awoke another, less abstract hunger. He wanted her; he wanted her soft body underneath him; he wanted her arms around him; he wanted the taste of her in his mouth. Bringing the list to a premature halt, he inhaled deeply and rose slowly to his feet.

How had he been in love and not seen it, refused to see it?

A memory from the past drifted like smoke through his mind.

'Why do you take her back?'

His father had shrugged in response to the angry question. 'I love her.'

'What is love?'

'A leap of faith.'

He had been so smug, so complacent, priding himself on his ability to be rational, to avoid messy emotional involvement. Now he could see that all that time he had not been rational, he had been afraid!

Afraid to take the leap of faith and end up where his father had. For the first time he thought of his father and did not feel anger and resentment, but pity. How different his life would have been if his leap of faith had taken him into the arms of a woman like Neve.

How many men were lucky enough to find a Neve? He had found her and discarded her. That made him…? Severo exhaled. That made him a man who had been given a second chance, and he was not going to waste it.

'This is a surprise.'

Neve walked into the middle of the room and stood uncertainly as he pushed his chair back from the big desk and rose to his feet. Behind him the glass-panelled wall revealed a stunning view of the City below.

Neve did register the view, but her heightened perceptions made her acutely aware of every detail of Severo's appearance.

As always his expression was hard to read; he looked big and tough and about the sexiest thing on two legs, but what went on behind those dark eyes?

To the casual observer he might appear composed, he carried himself with his habitual level of hauteur and arrogance, but Neve's interest was not casual. She saw the fine lines of strain bracketing his beautiful mouth and the hint of dark smudges under his incredible eyes.

She missed nothing, certainly not the tension rolling off him in waves. A swell of empathy swelled, making her throat ache as she imagined him alone, grappling through the long night with this dilemma. She wanted to rush across and hug him, but knew that such an action would not be appreciated.

She had to tread softly; his male pride needed careful handling. If he interpreted her actions as pity her brilliant plan would be dead in the water.

'I was passing, would you believe?'

He arched a brow. 'Frankly, no.'

Neve, her stomach twisting in tight tortuous knots of excitement, her heart thudding like a hammer, dropped her gaze from the blaze of molten heat she saw reflected in his dark eyes.

'I read somewhere that it's a good idea to choose your own battleground. I thought of waiting until I had you in bed. But—' she glanced around the enormous office '—there's more room here.'

'What exactly did you have in mind?' he asked, thinking about the feel of her body when it was pressed up tight against him, the way her bottom wriggled as she tried to get closer. Room was good, but at that moment his needs were so urgent that he'd have happily settled for a broom closet so long as she was in it!

'Actually—' Her eyes connected with the predatory gleam in his and the colour flew to her cheeks. 'Not that!'

He shrugged and smiled a dangerous smile that made her painfully conscious of the insidious progression of the liquid heat that had reached the apex of her trembling thighs. 'Pity.'

She struggled to focus through the fog of lust in her head. 'Look, I know you've got a lot on your plate at the moment and this might not seem the right time to discuss.'

It hit him then and he felt every kind of blind, besotted idiot he had always promised himself he would not be! He wanted her to be here because she had discovered she could not live without him; wanting did not make a thing so.

It was clearly much more likely that she had read the reports and she now thought he could not deliver on the promises of a life of luxury and lavish ease he had tried to sell her. It was tempting to fall back on his old protective cloak of wariness and cynicism but, looking at it logically, he was in no position to criticise.

It was logical for a woman to ensure that the man who had promised to take care of their child was able to do so.

'I very much want this discussion now,' he finally responded. 'It occurs to me that you might have read the newspapers today.'

'No, but Hannah rang me.' She scanned his face and struggled not to follow through with the very strong hugging impulse that flooded her. 'It's true, then?' She dropped her gaze, afraid of showing the sympathy that she was convinced he would automatically reject. 'I'm so sorry.'

'I am less of a catch than I was this morning.'

Neve's bewildered gaze flew upwards. It took her a second to take his meaning. 'Because you're broke, you mean?' She laughed; she couldn't help herself.

His jaw tightened. 'You find my straitened circumstances amusing? You have come to rub salt in the wound?'

The suggestion brought a spark of anger and hurt to her cornflower-blue eyes. 'No. I find the idea of women demanding to see your bank balance before they rip off their knickers and scream, "Take me," amusing,' she retorted.

Actually, now she was seeing it the image her blunt retort had conjured did not amuse her one bit. In reality it sent a stab of pure green jealousy through her body.

'That does not happen as often as reported.'

Her eyes fell from the amused gleam in his. 'You have to know that women are not going to care if you're stony broke, Severo.'

He flashed a cynical grin as his dark intense gaze moved over her upturned features. 'I would imagine it depends on the woman, *cara*.' There was only one woman's attitude he was interested in and as usual she was proving as unpredictable to him as her dress sense.

He looked so sad that she moved impulsively towards him, stopping just short of the big desk he stood behind and giving an awkward shrug and shuffling her feet.

'You look like a child who has been summoned to the headmaster's office.' He gave a discontented frown.

She lifted her chin and retorted, 'I'm not a child.' Though he showed a lamentable tendency to treat her like one—when he wasn't treating her like some sort of gold-digging trollop, that was.

His dark lashes swept downwards as his glance slid down her body, then lifted as he made a slow return journey back to her flushed face. By this point Neve, whose core temperature had jumped several degrees, was literally shaking like someone in the grip of a fever.

'This I am aware of, *cara*, but stop trying to deflect. Answer my question.'

Very conscious of the gleam in his eyes, she struggled to stay focused; not easy when your insides had dissolved. 'Me! I'm not trying to do anything.' Except keep my mind off the thought of your body naked. 'And you haven't asked a question—also, I wasn't summoned, I came,' she reminded him huskily. 'And if you must know it wasn't easy to get in.'

'You're pouting,' he said, sounding fascinated by the discovery as he stared at her mouth.

'You'd pout too. I thought at one point I was going to be strip-searched.' She lifted her hands wide and asked, 'Tell me, do I look like a terrorist or even a journalist?'

'Hmm, you do look somewhat suspicious.' His dark eyes glinted. 'Perhaps a strip-search is still not totally out of the question, *cara*.'

His glance swept downwards, the throaty growl half promise, or was it threat? Making the fine downy hair on her nape stand on end.

'So you managed to arrive fully clothed. Congratulations.'

He arched a dark sardonic brow and thought about correcting the situation.

Helpless to prevent his body from responding to the mental image of her slender, satiny curves, he cleared his throat before continuing, 'Now I recall the question—why exactly, if not to rub salt in the wound, did you come? Was it after all to give me my answer?'

She nodded. 'In a manner of speaking,' she admitted, her eyes sliding from his face as she looked around the room. 'This is a very nice office.'

'And very nice pictures on the wall, also big, but I am assuming you did not come to discuss the décor?'

Neve's gaze kept straying to the pulse that was ticking like a time bomb beside his mouth. It was not really surprising under the circumstances if he looked tense.

'Look, I know you probably don't want to hear this, but it's true money doesn't make you happy.' Her earnest blue gaze lifted to his face.

'So I have heard.' The lack of it, however, caused a lot of unhappiness. 'I have also heard the meek will inherit the earth, but I don't see it happening any time soon.'

'You're so cynical!' she protested.

'Guilty as charged,' he admitted. 'You ought to try it—it's safer in my opinion than always thinking the best of people.' It amazed him that he had ever compared her to Livia; the two women were poles apart in every way.

'I'll pass.'

'Now there's a surprise.'

Her eyes narrowed. 'I'm really not the gullible idiot you seem to think I am. I'm not saying it isn't very nice to have money to buy things, but the only rich person I knew was James and money was no help to him at the end.'

'You miss him?' Severo felt an unworthy stab of an emotion he remained reluctant to call jealousy.

Eyes misted, she nodded agreement. 'Look, I don't know if

this will help.' She retrieved the envelope from her bag. 'But you're welcome to it.'

Severo looked from the envelope she put on his desk and back to her face. He shook his head, a perplexed frown pleating his brow.

'What is this?'

Neve gave an awkward self-conscious shrug.

'I'm not using it, you might as well...' She shook her head, knowing she was fumbling the explanation, and finished crankily, 'Open it, don't just look at it!'

She watched as Severo did so, his actions seeming torturously slow to her as he slit the envelope with a silver-handled paper knife before sliding the contents onto his desk.

Tensely waiting his response, she watched his face through the mesh of her lashes as he read the figures, then he flashed her a hooded look through his dark eyes before seeming to read them again.

Without looking at her, he folded the paper and slid it back into the envelope.

'Well, what do you think?'

Few things surprised Severo, but the columns of figures on the page before him did. 'You are, it seems, a very wealthy woman.' If Neve agreed to be his wife it would not, it seemed, be for the luxuries he could provide.

'Yes.' She dismissed the comment with an impatient wave of her hand. 'But could you use it?'

'Could I use?' His confusion was not feigned.

'The money.'

Astonishment washed over him as her intention hit home. He swallowed, the muscles in his brown throat working as he forced the husky question past the emotional occlusion in his throat. 'You wish me to have your money?'

'Well, it's not mine...'

'You stole it perhaps, *cara*? To rescue me from my incompetence?'

'You're *not* incompetent,' she retorted sternly. 'So don't go all self-pitying on me because it's not a good look for you.'

His heart twisted in his chest as he looked at her, tasting the acrid bitterness of shame in his mouth. Her generosity humbled him and the knowledge that he had ever believed her to be selfish and avaricious, that he had ever believed he could buy her love, lay like a guilty weight in his chest.

He was not worthy of the love of a woman like this, but, *Dio mio*, he would be the luckiest man alive if he had it... Did he have it?

'Legally it is mine, of course it is.' Her brow furrowed as she struggled to explain her feelings about the unsolicited inheritance. 'But I've never really thought of it that way. I told James that I didn't want anything—what he had already given me was enough.

'I've no idea what sort of trouble financially speaking you are in. Would it be helpful until you get back on your feet? Which obviously you will.'

He was looking at her so strangely that she broke off and threw him a questioning look.

'You believe I can recover?'

She smiled, her blue eyes shining up at him. 'Of course you can. You can do anything you want,' she said with total conviction.

Severo shook his head. 'I hope so,' he said with shaken sincerity.

'I don't think you've thought this money-giving through, *cara*. Even if I—'

Sensing his rejection of her offer, Neve interrupted. She would not allow his stupid masculine pride to ruin her plan. 'Not *giving*,' she contradicted, flashing a winning smile.

'Never go into sales—it is not your thing.'

His attitude frustrated Neve. 'This is, it's...you can make it official, if you like. A loan?' Hearing the rising desperation in her voice she threw up her hands and yelled, 'I really don't care. All that money has done from day one is cause problems!'

The anguish in her voice drew a muffled oath from Severo, who reached her side before she had found the tissue she was fumbling for in her pocket.

He produced a man-sized handkerchief and after a moment Neve took it from him and blew her nose noisily.

'Hormones,' she muttered, not meeting his eyes as she handed it back.

Fighting back a grin, Severo said, 'Keep it, I have others.'

'So will you take the money?'

Severo shook his head. 'If I did that, Neve, people would say I had married you for your money and that would be very...hurtful?'

Their eyes met; the understanding she saw in his face made her throat ache. Tears standing out in her luminous eyes, she nodded. 'It would, but we're not getting married.'

'Because I'm a failure?'

'If you say stupid things like that I will hit you!' she promised fiercely.

Severo threw back his head and laughed as he placed his hands on her shoulders. 'I believe you, but you cannot stay in denial for ever.'

'I'm not in denial, and good to know you haven't suffered a crisis of confidence because you're having some cash-flow problems.' She huffed, 'This makes sense—you can pay me back, with interest if you like, and—'

He slid a hand into her wild red curls, tipping her head backwards as he stepped hard into her, pushing his thighs against her body. 'Shut up so I can kiss you.'

Shut up? She had dissolved the second she felt the rock-hard imprint of his erection against her belly. Before her distracted senses had even registered his throaty demand he had bent his head and was wrapping his arms around her, fitting his warm, firm mouth to her parted lips.

Neve's slim, supple body fitted itself to his hard, lean lines as she wound her arms around his neck and moaned into his mouth, responding with wild enthusiasm to the skilful, blissful hungry pressure of his lips.

A long moment later he lifted his head and sighed deeply. 'I needed that.' He cupped her face with a hand, spreading his fingers along her jaw. A possessive growl of appreciation vibrated in his throat as he repeated the sentiment with even more feeling. '*Really* needed that.'

Breathing in a series of gasps and still not sure if her feet were back on the ground, she nodded fervently in agreement, trying not to get too carried away by his comment. The kiss was a distraction, a respite from the troubles he was facing.

'You're a very good kisser, Severo.' Pretty good at everything actually.

Amusement gleamed in his eyes as he bowed his head in solemn acknowledgment of the compliment. 'Thank you, *cara mia.*'

Aware that she was probably sending out the wrong messages with her praise, she added quickly, 'But I still can't marry you.'

He arched a darkly delineated brow and struggled to contain his frustration behind a sardonic smile. 'You wish to marry a bad kisser perhaps?' Her refusal contradicted the message her body sent him every time he touched her.

Neve refused to smile back. Instead she took the hands that were now around her waist—God, but they felt so good there—and removed them before stepping backwards, not intending to but somehow retaining a hold of one of his hands. Her knees sagged as he wound her fingers into his and lifted her hand to his mouth.

The brush of his lips over the skin of her palm sent an electric jolt through her body.

'It's not a joke,' she protested, thinking, It's torture.

'I am not laughing.'

He wasn't. He was looking at her with a driven intensity that made it hard for her to remember why she couldn't marry him.

He doesn't love you!

The timely reminder made her wince.

'I really do understand how you feel about being a father. And you were right when you said a child needs two parents, and I agree a parent does need to put the needs of their child before their own, but I can't...' she said, shaking her head. 'I simply can't do it. I can't settle.'

The fingers linked with her own tightened so hard that she gasped in pain. Severo gave a grimace of apology but retained her fingers in a light grasp as he jerked her towards him, causing their bodies to collide.

It was not the force of the impact that drove the air from Neve's lungs, it was the thrill of being in close contact with the lean, hard length of him. Every square inch of her skin tingled; his sheer maleness was overwhelming, intoxicating and dangerously addictive.

Unable to resist the temptation, she pressed her face into his chest, breathing in the scent of his body.

Severo struggled to control several conflicting impulses as he gazed down at the bright head pressed to his heart. 'Marrying me would be *settling*? This is not a term I am familiar with,' he lied through clenched teeth.

A muscle clenched beside his lean jaw as she shook her head mutely and burrowed even closer into him, unable to bring herself to break the contact even though she knew she should.

'You consider me second best to what or who? I seem to recall that you told me several times that I *was* the best.'

Hands curled into his shirt, she tilted her head back and looked into his face. The tears trickled unchecked down her cheeks. 'I've offended you. But you *are* the best, but this isn't about sex. I'm not actually a very sexual person.'

This solemn declaration drew a burst of laughter from Severo. 'You don't believe that, Neve.'

Her eyes fell from the challenge in his. 'I did before I met you.' Emotion swelled in her chest and she pushed it away, saying, 'That's not relevant. You're not offering to marry me to get me into bed—you don't have to.' She slipped into his bed every night; it allowed her to maintain the illusion of freedom, but it had become a freedom she no longer wanted.

Astonishment flashed across his face. 'Are you offering to be my mistress but not my wife?'

'Isn't that what I am already? This isn't about what I'm offering. *You're* offering marriage because of the baby. Well, the thing is I've done the convenient marriage thing once. This time I want the real thing. Maybe it does make me selfish,' she admitted. 'But it's true.'

'You don't know the meaning of selfish.' How had he ever thought otherwise? 'You are an innocent. The world, *cara*, is a dangerous place for innocents.' He looked into her face and felt a rush of love so intense that it felt as if a hand had reached inside his chest. Miraculously she had survived until he came along without someone taking advantage of her generous trusting nature—it really was a mystery. 'You need someone to keep you safe.'

'Oh, Severo,' she choked, reaching for the handkerchief. 'That's such a lovely thing to say, but you don't have to say things like that. We'll work something out and—'

'If I take the money will you marry me?'

'It doesn't work that way. You're welcome to the money.'

He framed her face with his hands. 'I don't need the money. I need you.'

Neve closed her eyes, wishing with every fibre of her being that she could allow herself to take what he said at face value.

'And I need to marry for love.'

'Then do.'

She looked up at him, confusion written in her pale features. 'How is that possible?' she whispered, not daring to believe what she was seeing in his face.

'Marry me, Neve. Marry me because I love you.'

She looked at him through the tears that trembled on her eyelashes and shook her head, not daring to believe what he was saying.

'Is it possible?' she asked wistfully.

'It is impossible for me not to love you!' he declared. 'I prided myself on the fact I did not *need* any woman, and I was right. I do not need *any* woman, I need *you*, Neve and not just in my bed, though the sex with you is nothing short of miraculous. I need your face to be the last thing I see before I fall asleep. I need your face to be the first thing I see when I wake up. I need to hear your voice, your laugh. I need you in my life so I am asking you again. Marry me, Neve.'

'You always know what I am thinking so you already know that this time, Severo, the answer is yes.'

He pulled her into a crushing embrace. When they broke apart some time later he pushed her a little away from him and looked at her, his expression sombre.

'I think we should start as we mean to go on with no lies between us. With that in mind I feel I should confess.'

What was he going to say? A hundred possibilities ran through her head. She took a deep breath and, steeling herself for the blow to come, squared her shoulders.

'Tell me. It doesn't matter what it is, it won't come between us.'

'I'm very glad to hear you say that,' he admitted solemnly. 'The rumours in the paper.'

She gave a relieved sigh. 'Oh, it's just money. I thought it was serious.'

He grinned and said, '*Dio*, but I love you. No, I have to confess, *cara mia*, that the reports of my financial ruin have been slightly exaggerated.'

'Seriously—you're not broke?'

'Not even slightly,' he confessed with a grin.

'Then you don't need my money?'

He held open his arms and she stepped in, smiling as they closed tight around her, and Neve felt she had finally found her real home.

'The only thing I have ever needed is you.'

'I suppose you already know I feel the same way?'

'I have an inkling, but I think I'd feel happier if you showed me.'

Neve had no problem with this plan, none at all.

HIDDEN MISTRESS, PUBLIC WIFE
by Emma Darcy

Women fall at billionaire Jordan Powell's feet, so the challenge of seducing farm girl Ivy Thornton is a diverting amusement. But Ivy isn't prepared to be another disposable mistress...

THE FORBIDDEN INNOCENT
by Sharon Kendrick

Ashley Jones desperately needs her new job as formidable author Jack Marchant's assistant. Her heart goes out to her tortured boss—then one day they begin an affair that is as secret as it is forbidden...

THE SECRETARY'S SCANDALOUS SECRET
by Cathy Williams

When Luc Loughton discovers Agatha Havers' tantalising curves, awakening his wholesome secretary goes to the top of his agenda! Agatha is living the fairytale—until she's brought back to reality with a bump...

PRINCE VORONOV'S VIRGIN
by Lynn Raye Harris

Paige Barnes is rescued from the dark streets of Moscow by Prince Alexei Voronov—her boss's deadliest rival. Now he has Paige unexpectedly in his sights, Alexei will play emotional Russian roulette to keep her close...

On sale from 17th December 2010
Don't miss out!

Available at WHSmith, Tesco, ASDA, Eason
and all good bookshops
www.millsandboon.co.uk

JORDAN ST CLAIRE: DARK AND DANGEROUS
by Carole Mortimer

Helping aristocratic actor Jordan St Claire recuperate from an accident, physiotherapist Stephanie McKinley discovers the man behind the famous façade…and he's determined to unleash her reserved sensuality!

BOUND TO THE GREEK
by Kate Hewitt

Greek tycoon Jace Zervas hires Eleanor Langley—the flame he extinguished years ago—purely for business. But, secluded under the hot Mediterranean sun, Jace finds the fire of passion still burns…

RUTHLESS BOSS, DREAM BABY
by Susan Stephens

Magenta isn't expecting the old-fashioned ruthlessness of her new boss Gray Quinn! He'll give her the night of her life, but he might not be there when she wakes up… And he definitely doesn't want her taking maternity leave!

MISTRESS, MOTHER…WIFE?
by Maggie Cox

Dante Romano has fought hard to get where he is today—but nothing compares to discovering he's the father of a child. Marrying Anna Bailey is the only option to right the wrongs of the past…so he'll see her at the altar, willing or not…

On sale from 7th January 2011
Don't miss out!

Live life to the full - give in to temptation

Four new sparkling and sassy romances every month!

Be the first to read this fabulous new series from 1st December 2010 at **millsandboon.co.uk** In shops from 1st January 2011

Tell us what you think!
Facebook.com/romancehq
Twitter.com/millsandboonuk

Don't miss out!

Available at WHSmith, Tesco, ASDA, Eason and all good bookshops

www.millsandboon.co.uk

MILLS & BOON®

are proud to present our...

Book of the Month

St Piran's: Penhally's Wedding of the Year & St Piran's: Rescued Pregnant Cinderella

from Mills & Boon®
Medical™ Romance 2-in-1

ST PIRAN'S: THE WEDDING OF THE YEAR
by Caroline Anderson
GP Nick Tremayne and midwife Kate Althorp have an
unfulfilled love that's lasted a lifetime. Now, with their
little boy fighting for his life in St Piran's Hospital...can
they find their way back to one another?

ST PIRAN'S: RESCUING PREGNANT CINDERELLA
by Carol Marinelli
Dr Izzy Bailey is single and pregnant when she meets
the gorgeous neo-natal nurse Diego Ramirez. When
she goes into labour dangerously early Diego is there to
rescue her... Could this be the start of her fairytale?

Available 3rd December

Something to say about our Book of the Month?
Tell us what you think!

millsandboon.co.uk/community
facebook.com/romancehq
twitter.com/millsandboonuk

2 FREE BOOKS
AND A SURPRISE GIFT

We would like to take this opportunity to thank you for reading this Mills & Boon® book by offering you the chance to take TWO more specially selected books from the Modern™ series absolutely FREE! We're also making this offer to introduce you to the benefits of the Mills & Boon® Book Club™—

- **FREE home delivery**
- **FREE gifts and competitions**
- **FREE monthly Newsletter**
- **Exclusive Mills & Boon Book Club offers**
- **Books available before they're in the shops**

Accepting these FREE books and gift places you under no obligation to buy, you may cancel at any time, even after receiving your free books. Simply complete your details below and return the entire page to the address below. You don't even need a stamp!

YES Please send me 2 free Modern books and a surprise gift. I understand that unless you hear from me, I will receive 4 superb new books every month for just £3.30 each, postage and packing free. I am under no obligation to purchase any books and may cancel my subscription at any time. The free books and gift will be mine to keep in any case.

Ms/Mrs/Miss/Mr _____ Initials _____

Surname _____

Address _____

_____ Postcode _____

E-mail _____

Send this whole page to: Mills & Boon Book Club, Free Book Offer, FREEPOST NAT 10298, Richmond, TW9 1BR